The Price of
Three Stories

Photo of Hiroko Fujita and Fran Stallings is
provided by the National Storytelling Network

The Price of Three Stories

Rare Folktales from Japan

Hiroko Fujita & Fran Stallings

Parkhurst Brothers Publishers
MARION MICHIGAN

www.parkhurstbrothers.com

Parkhurst Brothers books are distributed to the trade through the Chicago Distribution Center, and may be ordered through Ingram Book Company, Baker & Taylor, Follett Library Resources and other book industry wholesalers. To order from Chicago Distribution Center, phone 800-621-2736 or send a fax to 800-621-8476. Copies of this and other Parkhurst Brothers, Inc., Publishers titles are available to organizations and corporations for purchase in quantity by contacting Special Sales Department at our home office location, listed on our website. Manuscript submission guidelines for this publishing company are available at our website.

Printed in the United States of America

First Edition, 2015
2015 2016 2017 2018 2019 2020   16 15 14 13 12 11 10
9 8 7 6 5 4 3 2 1

Library of Congress Cataloging in Publication Data: [Pending]

ISBN: Trade Paperback   978162491-061-6
ISBN: e-book   978162491-062-3

Parkhurst Brothers Publishers believes that the free and open exchange of ideas is essential for the maintenance of our freedoms. We support the First Amendment of the United States Constitution and encourage all citizens to study all sides of public policy questions, making up their own minds. Closed minds cost a society dearly.

Stories collected in Japan by	Hiroko Fujita
Edited and notes by	Fran Stallings
Cover and interior design by	Linda D. Parkhurst, Ph.D.
Proofread by	Bill and Barbara Paddack
Acquired for Parkhurst Brothers Publishers by:	Ted Parkhurst
Cover Photography by	Jessica Dowse

08015

Dedicated to the

listeners of all ages

in Japan and the United States
who have loved hearing Hiroko Fujita tell these stories;

and to the storytellers

who will continue to pass them on.

ACKNOWLEDGEMENTS

We thank Fujita-san's "Uncle in the Field," Mr. Kuni Takeda, and her elder colleague Mrs. Toshiko Endo, for preserving the folktales of Fukushima Prefecture, and for generously sharing them with her.

I heard many of these stories directly from Fujita-san during our travels together. My memory and journal notes were supplemented by English translations of story texts, which included many additional stories. For those texts I thank Fujita-san's followers, "The Young Yamanbas," who recorded and transcribed her tellings in Fukushima dialect. Taihou-sha Publishing Company (Tokyo) published the tales, along with traditional children's songs and games, as *Katare Yamanba* (Speak, Mountain Woman) volumes 1-7, 1996-2006. Makiko Ishibashi did most of the translation into English. A few stories were translated by Mitsuko Harada and Yoko Iwase. Michiyo MacMillan advised on pronunciation for the Glossary.

I am grateful for the comments and suggestions of Nikki Austin, Nancy Simpson, and my husband, Gordon Stallings, who read draft manuscripts. Story-loving friends kindly listened to me try to tell the stories orally, to test how much cultural information might be woven into the narratives.

We also thank the countless American schools, libraries, festivals and community centers that graciously sponsored our bilingual performances, especially Karen Morgan, who first let us test our tandem technique on her Library Sciences students at Texas Women's University, and Nancy Simpson, who helped arrange school visits in Stillwater, Okla., for our 12 American tours.

Many thanks for the tenacious and graceful staff at Parkhurst Brothers Publishers: to Ted Parkhurst for sharing our vision of these books, for Bill and Barbara Paddack, our tireless proofreaders, and to Susan Harring for her design skills and patience.

And we thank all people who love stories! Their enthusiasm has encouraged us to get translations of these rare tales into print.

Last but not least—our patient families, who didn't complain too much when we took off for another tour or spent time with our keyboards. We thank them for their support and encouragement.

CONTENTS

PREFACE

All the stories in this book come from the memory and telling of Hiroko Fujita.

She grew up in Miharu, a small farm town in the mountains of *Fukushima* Prefecture, Japan, hearing old folktales from village elders and classmates. When she became a teacher, she remembered the old stories and shared them with her students. Japanese adults also loved her stories, and asked her to print them in books. Now you can read them, too.

She wasn't born in that mountain town, but in Tokyo. She had just started first grade when her father decided the city was too dangerous for his family. It was 1941: Japan had entered the Second World War. He chose Miharu village although they had no friends or relatives there, but because he loved its beautiful name which means "Three Springtimes." Indeed, sometimes Miharu's plum, peach, and cherry trees all bloom at once! He hoped it would be a safe and beautiful home for his family until the war was over.

Their three-room cottage was crowded with Hiroko, her three older brothers, mother, and grandmother. Father had to keep running the family business in Tokyo and could only visit once a month. Sometimes an aunt and her family, or an uncle and his family, stayed with them, too. And after a while there was a new baby sister. When Hiroko wasn't at the village school, she played outdoors to escape that crowded house. That's how she met her "Uncle in the Field," an old farmer named Kuni Takeda, who didn't mind when little Hiroko came out to sit with him every time he took a rest break. And he was delighted that she loved stories. He had stories to tell.

Mr. Takeda was at least in his fifties in 1941. He had learned these stories when he was a boy, before 1900. If his teller was likewise fifty or sixty years old, that person would have learned the stories around 1853, the year when Japan rejoined the outside world after centuries of self-imposed isolation. So we think these stories are old indeed. She heard—and remembers—hundreds of them.

Returning to Tokyo in time for high school, she then attended Japan Women's University, training in early childhood education. She continued teaching after she married Dr. Toshi Fujita, had three children, and moved to Fukushima City where she met an elder lady from the same mountains. Mrs. Toshiko Endo knew hundreds of the same stories—and more. She shared over four hundred tales with Mrs. Fujita, two hundred of which they were able to print in a Japanese book.

昔

I met Hiroko Fujita in 1993 when I was visiting my brother in Japan. She and I began working together in 1995, touring American schools, libraries, and festivals: a total of twelve national tours, including twenty-two states. In 1997 she began bringing me to Japan for reciprocal tours. The National Storytelling Network in 2003 presented us its International StoryBridge ORACLE Award for our work on both sides of the Pacific Ocean.

Traveling together, we traded lots of tales. When she told stories in America, I introduced her stories in English then she told in Japanese. When I told stories in Japan, she introduced my stories in Japanese and I told in English. In order to introduce each other at these performances and workshops, we learned a lot of each other's repertory. But we also traded stories just for fun, or to illustrate a point, or when we saw something that triggered a memory. These tales didn't always fit our performances, but they were good stories and I wanted fellow Americans to hear them some day.

昔

There are already English translations of a dozen or so favorite Japanese folktales such as Momotaro (Peach Boy), Little One Inch, The Old Man Who Made Trees Bloom, etc. I didn't want this book to duplicate what is already available. Here you'll find stories that have rarely or never appeared in English before. If you love folktales, or Japanese traditional culture, I think you will really like these.

Hiroko Fujita's friends helped me to translate her seven story collections and her collection of tales from Mrs. Endo. These translations languished in my computer for years. When I told her that I felt like "a dog in the manger," guilty for not sharing the stories, I had to explain that phrase.

Her response was immediate: "Feed those animals!"

Here are some of our audiences' favorite tales, and others besides. We love these stories and hope that you will enjoy reading them.

–Fran Stallings
Bartlesville, Oklahoma
January 2015

ABOUT THE STORIES: Sometimes, before a story begins, we give a little background information that we think will be helpful. At the end of some stories, Mrs. Fujita adds an interesting COMMENT, or I add a NOTE with more information. We also often have a TIP FROM FRAN for storytellers.

To help you say the Japanese words and sound effects, we show stressed syllables with capital letters. For more information, go to the GLOSSARY & PRONUNCIATION GUIDE at the end of the book.

昔

DESIGN NOTE: The symbol chosen to denote breaks in the text is a symbol that means "old time or long time ago."

Kanji was the first writing script in Japan. It was imported from China around the middle of the 6th century AD. The Japanese term "kanji" means "Chinese characters". Kanji are ideographs meaning that the whole character conveys a meaning rather than just a sound (as in the case of hiragana and katakana letters). Kanji were originally drawn as pictures from nature but gradually transformed to more general-ized representations.
(http://redfinchjapanese.com)

STORIES HEARD AND TOLD
By Hiroko Fujita

I am not a "storyteller" but a professional early childhood educator. I tell stories together with children's songs, hand-made toys, plays with fingers, plays with words, and so on as part of early childhood education. I want to transmit these things to children. I want to give them the experience of listening to stories as a really pleasant but, at the same time, very significant, experience.

I do not collect stories from books, but I tell stories I heard in my childhood, especially stories I heard from neighboring farmers cultivating their fields. Therefore, the origin of my stories is limited to Fukushima Prefecture, and I tell them orally in the Fukushima dialect. The enjoyable and memorable time in my childhood is the very source and starting point of my storytelling. What motivates my storytelling is my desire to give children the same kind of pleasure that I had during my childhood, because I am convinced that the content of the stories and the enjoyable experience of hearing them told in a loving voice is very important for the growth of children.

The stories I tell are mostly stories I heard when I was seven to twelve years old. My family lived in the small town of *Miharu* in Fukushima Prefecture. Mr. Kuni Takeda, a farmer who worked the farmland next to my house told these stories to me when he rested during his work in the field. When we saw a snake in the field, he started to tell stories like "Two Rival Snakes." When a frog with warts on its back came out of the ground, the farmer used to say, "This frog has just come out of the *juubako* (lunch box) of the old woman in that house," pointing to a house nearby. He also told me the story of "*Botamochi* Turning Into Frogs." Therefore, I believed for a long time that the old woman living in the house was a greedy woman, though I later found out that she was actually warm-hearted and generous.

My paternal grandmother used to tell stories of people bewitched by foxes. My mother's mother used to tell legends of great Samurai warriors, but warriors were not my interest, and I don't remember their stories. However, I remember children's songs that she taught me. My father taught me names of flowers and birds, and in such occasions he used to tell me stories about the origins of those names.

After my marriage, I moved to Fukushima City. There I heard a lot of old stories from elderly people, especially Endo Toshiko-san. Love stories are among those I heard in Fukushima City after I grew up. Now I can tell about four hundred stories.

I hope you will tell the stories in my books using your own words and your own heart.

VILLAGERS

In Japanese folktales, the main characters are often *Jisama* (old man, Grandpa) and *Basama* (old woman, Grandma). But at what age were they called Jisama and Basama?

In the old days, when a girl turned thirteen years old she visited the shrine and then had a party to make her debut. When she had menarche, her family brought red-bean rice to their neighbors. They often got married in their teens. And if a woman's daughters also got married in their teens, she could easily have grandchildren before she was forty. And that means that she could be Basama before she was forty.

But even if they didn't have a grandchild, men and women were still usually called Jisama and Basama before they were forty. Country life required hard outdoor work. They did not have modern medicines. Probably they looked old before their time.

These days, people live up to one hundred. Now people in their forties are still children with runny noses.

Contest of Silence

INSIGHT: *Manju cakes*, the size and shape
of small eggs, are made of sweet bean jam
wrapped in pastry.

Once upon a time, there were Jisama and Basama. They were
living happily together.

One day, a neighbor brought them some manju cakes.
There were one, two, three, four, five, six, seven.

"Wow! I love manju." Basama said and ate one, *amu, amu,
amu, amu.* (sound of chewing)

Jisama took one and ate it, amu, amu, amu, amu.

"Wow, it's a good manju," said Jisama.

Basama took another and ate it, amu, amu, amu, amu.
"Yes, nice manju, really," said Basama.

Jisama took another and ate it, amu, amu, amu, amu.

Again, Basama took another. "This filling is so sweet and
good. It's so delicious." Saying so, Basama went amu, amu, amu,
amu.

Jisama took another and ate it, amu, amu, amu, amu.

Basama wanted another, and was going to reach for it.
Then she stopped. "Oh, there is only one left. Jisama, please take
it."

But Jisama said, "No, you want it. You can have it."

"No, no, you want it too. Jisama, please."

"No, go ahead, Basama."

"No, no, you can have it, please."

"You eat it."

Then Basama said, "Jisama, let's play a game of silence and decide which of us will eat it."

Jisama agreed. "Once we start the game, we can't speak. Agreed? Are you ready?"

Jisama and Basama sat staring at the manju without a word.

Soon it got dark, but they remained silent.

A thief came by. "Oh, this house is dark. Nobody is at home. Is the door locked?"

He tried the door. It was open.

"Oh, how careless they are! A thief might come in. Hello? A thief is coming."

The thief came into the dark house,

> NUki ashi, SAshi ashi, shiNObi ashi. (sound
> of tip-toe walking)

> NUki ashi, SAshi ashi, shiNObi ashi.

Then, he saw somebody. "Yow, they are at home! I've got to run."

But he looked into Jisama's face. Jisama was silent.

"Why? He doesn't say anything. Oh, here's Basama! Does she say anything?"

But Basama didn't utter a word.

"Strange. They say nothing. Maybe they are sleeping with their eyes open."

The thief spread out his carrying cloth.

"Here's something, maybe Basama's extra kimono. I will take it. This may be Jisama's kimono. And this is his jacket. I will take this futon, too."

18

He took everything, from Basama's extra petticoat to their futons. Still, Jisama and Basama remained silent.

As the thief was about to leave with the big bundle on his back, he saw the manju between Jisama and Basama. "Before I go, why not taste that good looking manju?"

He looked Jisama in the face. Jisama didn't say anything. "Well, he's all right."

He saw Basama. She didn't say anything, either. "Well, she's all right too. So—," he reached for the cake.

Basama yelled "You can't take it!"

Surprised, the thief fell flat on his back, dropping the stolen goods. He fled the house.

And Jisama threw the manju into his mouth and ate it up, amu, amu, amu, amu.

Oshimai ("It is closed," a traditional story ending in Fukushima dialect.)

Crane and Tortoise

Once upon a time, there was a very rich family. When their only son got married, the celebration was very big. They invited many guests. In a great reception hall they put long lines of personal dinner tables crowded with dishes. In the *tokonoma* (alcove) behind the wedding couple, they put little statues of Okina & Oona, Jisama with a bamboo rake and Basama with a broom, to represent active old age and a long, healthy marriage. They also put little statues of *Tsuru* (crane) and *Kame* (tortoise) which represent

19

longevity, 1,000 and 10,000 years, respectively. Each guest sat at his personal table, ate, drank, sang, and danced. It was such a big celebration.

But it finally came to an end. One guest left. Then two left. Finally all the guests were gone.

In front of the figurines in the alcove, only the groom and the bride remained.

According to custom in the old days, they had never met. The groom had not even seen his bride's face, because it was hidden by a huge white headdress.

"What does my wife look like, I wonder?" he thought.

He peeked under the bride's headdress. What a beautiful bride! He became so happy.

"Uh ... hello. Everybody is gone. You don't have to sit so far away. Come closer."

The bride, kneeling on her cushion, said, "Oh, no. I'm too shy."

Still, she inched a little closer to her new husband.

"It's all right," he said. "There's nobody here but us. Come a little closer."

"Oh, no. I'm too embarrassed," the bride replied. Still, she came a little closer. "I'm meeting you for the first time this evening, and I feel shy." However, she moved a little bit toward the groom.

"There is nothing to worry about. Come a little bit closer to me," the groom said again.

"Oh, no. I'm too shy." Though she repeated the same thing, she moved closer and closer to the groom. Finally the newly wedded couple were very close together.

昔

The statues of Jisama and Basama were watching this from the alcove.

Jisama, holding his bamboo rake, said to his wife who was holding her broom, "Basama, Basama, look at them. How wonderful to be young! Look at how close they sit with each other. Honey! You don't need to hold the broom. Why don't you come closer to me?"

"What are you talking about, Jisama? Think of your age. Oh, well ..." she said, but she moved a little bit closer to her husband.

"You, too, think of your age. You are too old to be shy! Come a little bit closer," he said.

"Oh, you are so silly," but Basama came a little closer.

Finally, they, too, were close together.

昔

Crane and Tortoise were watching them.

Crane spoke to Tortoise. "Look at them. How wonderful to be young! Look at how close they are. Hey, Tortoise, I know you are not married yet. Will you become my wife?"

"No," Tortoise shook her head.

"Why? Is it because you don't like my long thin beak?"

"No, that's not the reason," replied Tortoise.

"Is it because you don't like my long, thin neck?"

"No, that's not the reason."

"Is it because you don't like these long, thin legs?"

"No, that's not the reason."

"So, why? What don't you like about me?"

"It's not that I don't like you. But if I marry you, I'll have to be a widow for 9,000 years," Tortoise replied.

Oshimai

昔

COMMENT FROM MRS. FUJITA: In old Japan, most marriages were considered to be the business of the two families, and the most important thing in the marriage was the agreement by the heads of the two families instead of the agreement of the marrying couple. Therefore, there were indeed cases where a bride and a groom saw each other for the first time at the wedding ceremony.

TIP FROM FRAN: If you act bold as the bride, who keeps saying "I'm so embarrassed" but still comes closer and closer, people will enjoy it very much. When I tell this, the contrast between my age and my frisky action seems to be funny, because it makes every listener laugh.

A Couple Married on Koshin Day

INSIGHT: In the old Japanese calendar, *Koshin* was number fifty-seven in the cycle of sixty days. On that day, three "worms" inside a person were believed to go up to heaven to inform on his sins while he was asleep. In order to avoid that, people used to stay awake all night. And a man and wife were not supposed to share a futon that night.

Once upon a time, there was a man who was very ugly. His nose pointed to the ceiling, his eyes crossed, his lips were as lumpy as cod roe. Because he was so ugly, he couldn't find a wife.

In a next village, there was a young woman. I don't know why, but her hair was all gone. She was bald. Nobody wanted to marry a bald woman. So, she couldn't find a husband.

They resigned themselves to not marrying. But there was a man who was very good at matchmaking. He went to the bald woman and said, "You know, in the next village, there is a good man. Wouldn't you like to marry him?"

"I would like to, but you see, I am bald. Will he marry me?"

"Of course! He said to me he won't be picky. You don't have to worry," he assured her.

"Then, I will marry," she said.

Then the matchmaker went to the ugly man in the next village. He said, "You know, there is a young woman in the next village. She has such beautiful hair, as black as a raven. Don't you want to marry her?"

The ugly man said, "Yes, I would like it very much. But I'm so ugly. Will she marry me?"

"She is a very kind woman. She won't mind. So, you don't have to worry," the matchmaker assured him.

昔

The man settled that they were to marry on Koshin Day the next month.

The bride wore a white headdress that was very deep, completely covering her face. The groom sat very far from the bride. They had the wedding ceremony and afterwards, the reception.

Relatives and neighbors were all invited. They drank and sang. It lasted all day. So it was already dark when the guests started going home.

And it was time for the couple to go to their room. In the dark room, they performed the three-times-three exchange of nuptial cups of *sake* (rice wine). In the dark, they removed their wedding finery and got into their futon. In the dark, they formed an intimacy.

And it was after midnight that a scary voice came from the ceiling.

"What a terrible thing you have done! You aren't allowed

23

to do that on Koshin Day! You broke the rule. I will have to take your lives, both man and woman!"

It was such a scary voice. Bride and groom shuddered together in the futon. "Please, please have mercy and spare our lives," they begged.

Then the voice from the ceiling said, "All right. I will spare you. But I will take all the hair from the bride. And as for groom, I will twist your nose up to the ceiling, make your lips lumpy like cod roe, and make you cross-eyed. Be prepared!"

The voice was gone.

昔

The next morning, the couple found out that the wife had no hair. The husband's nose was pointing to the ceiling, his lips lumpy and his eyes crossed.

"But," they agreed, "we are lucky we are alive."

They lived happily ever after.

Oshimai

Two in One Bite

Once upon a time, there was a young woman. Right before her wedding, her mother told her, "At your new home, don't eat a dumpling in one bite. It's bad manners."

Her daughter said, "Yes, mother!"

At her new home, she remembered what her mother had told her.

She didn't eat a dumpling in one bite. She ate two dumplings in one bite.

Oshimai

Sewing Lesson

Once upon a time, there was a young daughter-in-law. Her mother-in-law handed her new cloth and told her, "With this cloth, sew a loincloth for your husband."

But this daughter-in-law was not so good at sewing. Night after night, she tried. She sewed some, but undid it. She sewed again, but again she undid it. She wasn't getting anywhere.

Her mother-in-law couldn't stand it any longer. "Give that to me," she said. And she sewed the loincloth in a few minutes.

Then the daughter-in-law said to her, "Oh, Mother, you could sew so fast. Thanks to the holes I made night after night, it was easy sewing, wasn't it?"

Oshimai

Unhappy Daughter-in-Law

Once upon a time, there lived Jisama, Basama, and their son. They were having a hard time finding a wife for the son. He was somewhat weak in the head, but not totally a fool. Finally, someone in their village arranged a wife for him.

The young wife was told all sorts of nice things about her future husband, but she found out those were not so true. She thought, "Oh, no! I was tricked into marrying a fool!"

She wasn't very happy. "I don't want to stay here. I'll try to be dismissed."

When she cooked rice, she deliberately scorched it. When she made soup, she made it either too strong or too thin. She tried hard not to cook good food.

We don't know if her mother-in-law knew what the young woman was thinking, but she didn't scold her daughter-in-law at all. "Oh, today's miso soup is a little bit salty. But salty miso soup is good, because you can work hard and sweat and still you will be all right."

When the soup was too weak, she would say, "Today's soup is weak, for the elderly."

When served the scorched rice, she would say, "This scorched rice tastes rather good." She poured soy sauce on it and ate it up. She wouldn't dismiss her daughter-in-law.

昔

Soon, it was summer. In summer, they had to weed their rice fields. It was very hard work. They were covered with sweat. The prickly ears of rice stung their faces. Their backs ached. The daughter-in-law thought, "Day after day, we have to weed in our rice field. This is so hard."

Then she got an idea. "Yes! When I weed, I will stir up the mud very hard. The rice plants will fall down. Their roots will be cut off. They will think I am a very bad wife and they will dismiss me."

But when autumn came, it turned out that they got a rich harvest. When you weed in the rice field, if you stir up the mud very hard, fresh air gets into the water and the plants take strong root. And that produces a good harvest.

Basama said, "Oh, my daughter-in-law is such a hard-working wife. She doesn't spare herself when she weeds. She stirred up the mud deeply, so the rice plants took strong root. And we got a good harvest. We got a nice wife for our son. She is a good wife."

昔

In the autumn, when the young wife peeled the persimmon skin too thick, Basama said she could add the skin to the pickles to make them sweeter. When she peeled the potato skin too thick, Basama said she could feed it to the rabbits and chickens. For everything she did, Basama praised her. The wife couldn't find any chance to go back home.

Finally she realized she was lucky to have such a kindly mother-in-law. She lived with Basama happily ever after.

Oshimai

昔

COMMENT FROM MRS. FUJITA: In the old days, a young wife had to obey her mother-in-law until she inherited full responsibility to run the house. It was more important to please her mother-in-law than her husband, because it made her living much easier.

After ten or fifteen years, the older woman had to "hand over the rice scoop" to her daughter-in-law. Then the daughter-in-law became the housewife of the family. The housewife was in charge of money, not Basama. Basama couldn't spend as much money as she wanted for her own daughters who were married into another family. That's why women didn't want to hand over the rice scoop easily.

People didn't waste anything in old days. Persimmon peels made pickles sweeter. They dried orange peels and put them in the bath water. My mother used to wipe her hands and face with apple peels when there was no cream. After each use, everything was put in the compost and made into a fertilizer.

Eavesdropping Mother-in-Law

Once upon a time, there was a very strict mother-in-law. She scolded the new bride of the house for everything she did: how she used her chopsticks, how she took off her sandals, and even how she walked. When her daughter-in-law finished cleaning the house, the mother-in-law checked the *shoji* (paper-covered screen) frame with her finger and blew the dust off.

The bride couldn't eat her supper until all the workmen finished theirs. She couldn't take a bath until everybody else did. So, when it was finally her turn, the water was only up to her knees and it was lukewarm. Of course she had to work in the vegetable field and rice field. Also, the mother-in-law made her do all the uncomfortable jobs such as tending the fire in hot summer, and fetching water in cold winter.

One day, she was crying on the veranda. "My mother at home was so kind. When I wanted to weave, she set up the warp for me. In summer, she asked me to fetch water. In winter, she asked me to watch the fire. I could eat supper while the food was still warm. When we had napa cabbage pickles, she put the best part on my plate. Now I must call both of these women "Mother." But this mother here is so mean and strict. She is like an *Oni* (ogre). How was she when she was young?" She was talking aloud to herself.

The door behind her suddenly slid open and her mother-in-law peeked out. She said, "A mother-in-law isn't an

Oni or a snake. She was once a bride herself. She is just the old daughter-in-law."

Oshimai

昔

Comment from Mrs. Fujita: In the old days, it seems that every mother-in-law was strict and mean. Mothers-in-law had the responsibility to train girls to become "full women." They had to become like Oni to do that. Then, that young wife became another Oni to train the next wife of the house. It was sort of a training system. Thanks to the strict mothers-in-law, young women grew stronger and wiser.

If someone says, "That girl was brought up watching fire in winter," it means that the girl was brought up indulgently. Of course, we had to watch fire throughout the year. Suppose a mother says, "I am being fair. I make both my daughter and my daughter-in-law watch the fire and fetch water." But she may be making her daughter-in-law watch fire in summer and her own daughter in winter. In order to become "full women," girls have to watch fire in summer and fetch water in winter, too.

Today, mothers spoil their daughters. And mothers-in-law are so weak-kneed. Girls don't watch fire even in winter. Where do they learn to become "full women?"

Poisoning Her Mother-in-Law

Once upon a time there was a young wife. Every day, she was scolded by her mother-in-law. This mother-in-law complained about everything she did, how she used her chopsticks, how she swept the floor. This mother-in-law even went around talking ill of her.

29

The young wife thought, "I can't live with her any more. Either she dies or I die. Anyway, I don't want to live like this."

She went to the priest and explained to him. "Do you have any good ideas?" she asked.

The priest answered, "If your mother-in-law is so mean, it is best to kill her. You want to kill her, don't you?"

She nodded.

"I see. Take this powder here. Sprinkle a very tiny pinch on her rice every day for a hundred days. I guarantee you she will die on the hundredth day. But you know, if a healthy woman like her dies suddenly, people might suspect that you killed her. To avoid that, you have to be very obedient to her for these hundred days. If she says it's black, it's black, even if it's white. Just agree with her. Always think of something that makes her happy and do it for her. Always prepare dinner that you think she likes." The priest taught her and she went back home.

"Well, if it's only for a hundred days, I can stand anything."

昔

Every morning and night, she sprinkled a tiny pinch of the powder on her mother-in-law's rice. And she followed the priest's instruction.

"Mother, mother, shall I massage your back?" She gave her a massage.

She woke up earlier than her mother-in-law and prepared breakfast. She prepared a hot bath and asked her mother-in-law to take it first. When she got something, she always brought the biggest one to her mother-in-law. Whatever the mother-in-law said, she always agreed with her. Her answer was always, "Yes, mother." And she obeyed her orders.

Fifty days passed, and sixty days passed. The mother-in-law

started to feel strange. She had complained about almost every-thing the young wife did, even how she used chopsticks. But now, she was going around bragging about her. "Our daughter-in-law is really a kind girl."

When she got something, she gave half of it to her daugh-ter-in-law. At night, she said, "You must be tired. You can go to sleep before I do."

Ninety days passed, then, ninety-five, ninety-six, and ninety-seven. Now, every day, the mother-in-law was very kind to her. The young wife no longer felt like killing her. "She is such a kind mother-in-law. If I kill her, I will surely go to hell. Before she dies ..."

She hurried to the priest. "Oh, Priest, please. If my moth-er-in-law is dying, I must die first. I want another packet of that powder," she begged him. "I will swallow it all at once and die. I'm going to heaven with my mother-in-law."

And the priest told her. "That powder was only sugar. You don't have to worry."

Oshimai

An Offering Withdrawn From Buddha

Once upon a time, there was a young couple. They loved each other very much.

When they worked in the vegetable field, they worked together. When they went to a mountain to collect wood, they went together. When they did tasks at night, they worked together.

31

Such a loving couple they were.

But one day, I don't know why, the husband passed away suddenly. The wife was so surprised and sad, but somehow held a funeral for him.

Until then, she always slept with her husband. But now she had to sleep alone. She felt very lonely.

Every night, she cried in her futon. "Oh, I miss him. I miss him."

One night, the young wife was crying in her futon as always. The shoji door slid open quietly and she saw her husband standing over there!

"Oh, my! You came back! Please, please, come in to our futon."

· But her husband just stood at the shoji door, very pale, and didn't move.

"Oh, please come in."

The wife went toward him, but then he disappeared.

"Oh, no! He must have come here with much trouble, but he is gone."

Next day, again at midnight, the shoji door slid open quietly and the husband was standing over there.

"Please, please come to futon."

She called but he just stood there. She stood up and went toward him. But then, again, he disappeared.

It was the same every night, again and again. Every night the husband came to her, and she couldn't sleep well.

昔

So she went to talk to the priest. She explained everything and asked him, "What should I do?"

The priest replied, "You know, your husband is still attached to something on earth and can't go to Paradise yet. You should hold a proper service for him or he won't be able to go to Paradise. I will read a sutra for him tomorrow. Please bring an offering of something that your husband loved most."

昔

The wife went home and thought, "Well, what did my husband love most? Yes, it's *botamochi* (rice snacks covered in bean jam). He loved botamochi very much."

She made botamochi early the next day. She brought them to the temple. The priest offered the botamochi in front of the Buddha statue. He chanted the sutra,

Nanmaida. Nanmaida. Nanmaida. Nanmaida.

Then, he took the botamochi down from the altar.

"An offering withdrawn from Buddha must be shared by the person who brought it and the priest. That's the proper service. So, let's eat this botamochi together."

The two of them ate botamochi together.

"He won't be back tonight," assured the priest.

昔

But that night again around midnight, the shoji door slid open quietly and the pale husband was standing there, not moving. She called but he didn't come. She went toward him, but he disappeared again.

The next day, the wife went to the priest again. "Priest, priest, it was no good. We held a service for him yesterday, but he came back again last night."

The priest said, "You know, that's because you misunderstood what he loved most. Didn't he have something else he loved more than botamochi?"

Then the wife said, "Oh, that's right. My husband loved sake. I will bring sake here."

33

She ran home, and brought back a bottle of sake. They offered the sake to Buddha.

Nanmaida. Nanmaida. Nanmaida.
Nanmaida.

He chanted the sutra and withdrew the offering. The priest and the wife drank sake together.

"He won't be back tonight," assured the priest.

昔

But that night, again around midnight, he appeared.

So the next day, the wife thought again. "That's right! My husband loved sushi. I will make *chirashi-zushi* (vinegar-soaked rice mixed with bits of vegetables, egg, and other good tidbits) and bring it today."

She made chirashi-zushi and brought it to the temple.

"Priest, priest, he came back again last night. I thought again, and I think what my husband loved most was chirashi-zushi. Please offer this and do the service for him."

They offered the chirashi-zushi to Buddha.

Nanmaida. Nanmaida. Nanmaida.
Nanmaida.

They withdrew it and the two of them shared it together.

"He won't be back tonight," assured the priest.

昔

But he came back again. The next day, the wife thought and thought. "Oh, yes!"

She ran to the temple. "Priest, priest, he came back again last night. And I thought very hard. Today I want to offer something he loved the most."

"Oh, yes? But first, I have things to do in my living room. So please offer it there and wait for me."

The priest went to his living room and finished what he had to do. Then he returned.

He saw the wife sitting in a strange position, a position used only for intimacy. The priest asked the wife, and she said, "My husband loved botamochi. He loved sake and sushi, too. But he didn't have them every day. What he loved every day was this."

"I see. I see. Now, I will read a sutra."

He sat in front of her and chanted, "Nanmaida. Nanmaida. Nanmaida. Nanmaida."

He read a sutra and said, "Now, let's withdraw the offering and share it."

They shared it and the wife went home.

昔

That night, her husband didn't come back.

After that, the wife went to the temple occasionally and held the service.

And the husband never came back. Maybe he went to Paradise.

Oshimai

昔

COMMENT FROM MRS. FUJITA: For a young widow, the young priest who could share her "offering" was better than the ghost husband who could only stare at her.

I came to like sensual stories after I heard them from Toshiko Endo. Maybe one reason was that I was then adult, and could appreciate such stories. Also, her telling was light. Some might not understand the meaning, but still could enjoy the story.

Sensual stories are harder to tell than other stories. Some tellers are too explicit, and listening to them becomes almost painful. So, I try to tell them elegantly. But maybe I'm not that seasoned yet. There are many stories I can't tell yet.

Please

Once upon a time, there was a wife. She was working in the storage house alone.

A handsome young farm worker came. He stood at the door, looking nervous.

"Do you have something to tell me?" asked the wife.

"Yes, I want to ask you something."

"What? Tell me."

"But it's not so easy ... May I come in?"

"Yes, if you have something to tell me, come in."

"Well, then."

The farm worker came in. He said he didn't want to say it in a loud voice, so he came closer. Then, he started whispering into her ear. "I have something to ask you."

"What?"

"I've always thought I would tell this someday. I've always wanted you to know how I felt. When should I tell? When ...? I was waiting for this opportunity."

The wife started to feel warm.

"Please allow me to tell you this now. I ... I ..."

Waiting for his words, the wife closed her eyes.

"I ... I'm always hungry. Please scoop a little more rice into my bowl."

Satisfied, he went out of the storage house.

Oshimai

The Price of Three Stories

INSIGHT: *Ryo*, equal to about 1,000 yen (about ten dollars US now), was an oval gold coin in the Edo period.

Once upon a time, there was a man who worked in a town far away from his home. He made one hundred Ryo a year. After three years in the town, he asked for leave. They paid him three hundred Ryo and with that money in his jacket, he headed for his home.

On the way home, he saw a shop which had a sign: "We sell stories."

"Oh, I have a lot of money now. I'll buy a few stories and go home."

He entered the store. Inside the store, there was a sign: "Part one, one hundred Ryo."

"I don't know how many stories I can get with one hundred Ryo. That's one year's salary! But I will try it. I have three hundred Ryo with me. It should be all right if I use one hundred." He paid one hundred Ryo.

A storyteller came out. "Now, this is part one." And he said, "Don't rest where there is no column. Don't rest where there is no column."

"I see. He is going to tell me the story called, 'Don't Rest Where There Is No Column.'"

The man waited. But the storyteller said, "That's all."

"What? Is that all? But I can't explain to my family that that's the story I bought. I have to hear some stories I can tell them."

He saw a sign, "Part two, another one hundred Ryo." He paid it and asked, "Please tell me the next one."

The storyteller said, "All right, this is part two. Don't stay where sweet words are."

"Oh, now, he is going to tell me the story called, 'Don't Stay Where Sweet Words Are.'"

He waited. There was a long silence. And the storyteller said, "This is the end of part two. The end."

"What? Is that all? I can't tell that to my family. I see a sign, 'The final part, another one hundred Ryo.' What is that?" asked the man.

"It's another one hundred Ryo. Is it OK?" asked the storyteller.

"Yes," answered the man.

"All right then, I'll tell you. Endure what you can't endure. Endure what you can't endure. The end."

He had used up all the money he had earned in the last three years to buy three sentences!

He headed for home.

"I don't want to forget the stories I paid for." So, he chanted them as he walked.

"Part one is, don't rest where there is no column. Part two is, don't stay where sweet words are. And the final one is, endure what you can't endure. These cost me three hundred Ryo. I think that's rather expensive."

He walked for a long time. He was just getting tired when it started raining.

"Oh, I had better take shelter somewhere and rest for a while."

He looked around. He saw a big rock cave. "I will take a rest here."

He went in and sat down.

"What were the stories I bought? Let's see if I can remember them."

He tried. "Don't rest where there is no column. Oh, there is no column here! I shouldn't rest where there is no column. I shouldn't." Though it was still raining a little, he dashed out of the cave.

Suddenly, a big earthquake shook the ground.

> *Gura, gura, gura, gura.* (sound of the earth shaking)

And the cave collapsed down.

"Phew! That was close! Well, that story was worth one hundred Ryo or more!"

昔

And he went on. The sun had set. He had to decide where to stay that night. He saw two inns. At one of them, a grumpy-looking Basama was sitting at a desk. She didn't say, "Please come in. Please stay here," or anything. Silently she just sat there.

From the other inn, a beautiful woman came out and pulled his sleeve saying, "Please come in. Please stay here."

"Oh, it'll be much nicer to stay here than at that other inn."

So, he went into the inn with that beautiful lady. She took him to a beautiful room. "Dinner should be ready soon. Well, well, you must be tired." She gave him a shoulder massage, and folded his kimono.

"She is so nice!" He was feeling very good.

"Where are you from? That's great. Shall I give you a foot massage?" And she did. "Now, your dinner should be ready." Saying so, she went out of the room.

He looked around. It was a big room, with a chest, a mirror, and many things. There was even a kimono hanger. "I'm lucky to stay here."

He looked at the soft comfortable silk futon. "This is a wonderful room."

Then, he remembered the stories.

"Don't rest where there is no column. That was the first one. Don't stay where sweet words are. That is the second story. But this lady was so nice to me. Should I really be staying here?"

He felt somehow uneasy and dashed out of the room.

Suddenly, its suspended ceiling fell down.

"If I had stayed there, I would have been as flat as a cracker," he thought. "I can't stay here."

He went to the inn across the street with that unfriendly Basama. He could stay there safely.

昔

Early next morning he left there, and finally arrived back at his house.

He slid the door open and called, "I'm home!" But there was no answer.

"That's strange. Where is my wife? I heard that my mother is not feeling well. My wife wouldn't leave my sick mother alone. Is my mother not here either? Nobody says anything."

He went inside. Through a slightly opened sliding door, he could see into the bedroom. He saw the futon. His wife was in the futon. She wasn't alone. It looked like two people were in the futon.

40

"Oh, no! While I was gone, my wife took a lover into my house!" In a rage, he pulled out his dagger. "I will stab them."

But then, he remembered the last story.

"Endure what you can't endure. That's right. Endure what you can't endure."

He remained where he was and waited. Soon, his wife crawled out of the futon, opened the sliding door and came to him.

"Welcome home! These days, your mother isn't feeling well. She can't take a nap unless I lie down with her until she falls asleep. I heard your voice, but she was just falling asleep. I was afraid if I called back, she would wake up, so I remained silent. I'm sorry," she explained.

"Thank goodness!" he thought. "I almost killed this wonderful wife of mine. One hundred Ryo for that story was really, really cheap."

He told his wife what had happened. They both were very thankful.

Oshimai

TRICKSTERS

Fleas on a Skewer

Once upon a time, there was a traveler who stayed one night at an inn. Probably it was the rainy season, when fleas are abundant. When he stretched out in his futon, he felt a flea bite.

"Ow! A flea bit me."

He tried to scratch it, then felt another flea bite on his thigh. "Ow! Another bite!"

Then he felt another one on his behind. "My, my! Another one!"

Then he felt another on his stomach. On his neck, back, chest, and everywhere, he got flea bites, and he couldn't sleep a bit.

In those days when there were no cars or trains, traveling meant walking all day. So he was very tired and sleepy. But every time he started to doze, he felt a flea bite!

He stretched out his legs. He drew in his legs. He rolled over this way. He rolled over that way. Though he tried, he couldn't get any sleep.

昔

Finally it was morning. Rubbing his puffy eyes, he went to

the dining room. By the hearth sat Basama stirring miso soup in a big pot. She asked, "Did you sleep well?"

The man didn't know what to say, so he just grumbled, "You have plenty of fleas here."

"I think we do," said Basama calmly.

"Hmmm," the man thought, "this woman really doesn't care."

He sat by the hearth and ate the thin soup with just a few bits of vegetables in it. Then he said aloud, but as if he was talking to himself, "What a pity! There are so many fleas here. I could make a lot of money with them. But I have no time to collect them now. What a pity!"

Basama's eyes sparkled. "Excuse me, sir. Can you make money with fleas?"

"Yes, I've heard so," answered the man.

"How do you make money with them?" asked Basama.

"I don't know how it's done. But I've heard they make good medicines. So drug stores in the city collect them. There are no fleas left in the city any more. So now they are asking people, people like me who travel a lot, to find fleas. They said they would pay for the work. But I have to get going, and have no time to collect the fleas here."

He told her, "Well, thank you for the breakfast."

He put on his sandals and prepared to leave. "Thank you. And so long," he said and was about to leave when Basama stopped him.

"Excuse me, sir. Are you stopping here again on your way back?"

"Yes, this is the only route I can take. I suppose I will be here again," the man replied, and left.

昔

As soon as he left, Basama turned round and went straight into the house. She turned over the old futon. She tore off the old straw coverings on the *tatami* floor mats. Tucking up her sleeves with a sash, she knelt down and started to catch fleas. All day long Basama caught fleas, doing nothing else, with her bottom sticking up toward the ceiling.

昔

After some days, the man came back to the inn. This time he found it very comfortable. There was not one flea! He stretched out his arms and legs and slept deeply. The next morning he was so refreshed. Feeling wonderful, he went to the dining room smiling happily.

Basama at the hearth was smiling happily, too. She served rice and soup for him. This time, the soup had many delicious tidbits. The rice bowl was heaping full. "Eat more. Eat more. How about a second bowl of soup?" asked Basama.

He was not a man to hesitate. So he asked for another and another until he became very full. After breakfast, as he was drinking the hot water that is used to clean the bowls at the end of the meal, Basama stood up, went to the closet, took out a bucket and carried it to the man.

She put it right beside him and said, "Sir, will you look at this?"

To his surprise, the bucket was three quarters full of dead fleas. "Wow, Basama, you collected a lot of fleas. You took my word and really collected them!" said the man.

Basama looked at him sharply and said, "Yes, I caught them. So tell me how much this would be worth."

"Sorry, Basama. This is worth nothing."

"What? Nothing? You thought I was stupid and told me a lie to make me catch fleas?" Basama accused him with flaring eyes.

44

"No, no, I didn't tell you a lie. I just didn't tell you the whole story. I don't know why, but you can't make medicine with male and female fleas together. So before you take them to a drug store, you have to divide them between male and female, and skewer them ten by ten. Otherwise they won't take it. I'm sorry I just told you half the story, but you didn't tell me that you were going to catch them."

Basama couldn't even stand up. She just sat there.

"Basama, Basama, don't get discouraged. Remember, next time you catch fleas, you divide them into male and female and skewer them ten by ten. Then, I will take them to the city and sell them for you.

"Until then, thank you very much," the traveler said, and left.

Oshimai

昔

COMMENT FROM MRS. FUJITA: When I was a child, every child had fleas and lice. After the U.S. occupation forces gave orders to spray us with DDT (a chemical insecticide, prohibited in 1971), these vermin gradually diminished.

I was a very good flea catcher. Maybe I was a bad athlete, but I was quick when I was catching fleas. Keeping time with the flea's hopping, I pressed it down with my finger. While I crushed it between my thumbnails, I was looking for another flea. Doesn't it sound like I was an expert?

The Bridge Officer

Once upon a time there was a Jisama who absolutely loved to drink sake. But he was very poor and couldn't afford sake whenever he wanted. He worked hard and saved money, and when he had saved enough, with an empty bottle in his hand and some coins in his pocket, he walked to the wine shop that was located in the neighboring town, across the river.

A bridge officer kept watch, on the lookout for suspicious persons crossing between towns.

When Jisama passed the officer in the morning, he greeted him with a polite "good morning" but the officer only grunted. Jisama went on his way to the wine shop, had his bottle filled up to the top with sake and, carrying the heavy bottle, headed eagerly home.

When he came to the bridge, he bowed to the officer and said the traditional "thank you for doing your job." He was about to continue on his way when the officer stopped him.

"Mister, you are not at all suspicious. I know very well that you live in this town. But the contents of that bottle seem suspicious. Give it to me, I will examine it."

"No, no, this is nothing suspicious. This is just some sake."

"I doubt whether it's really just wine. Give it to me, I will examine it," he said, and grabbed the bottle out of the old man's hand. He removed the lid and *gokku gokku gokku* (swallowing sound) drank it almost all up. "Yes, just as you said, it really was sake. It wasn't anything suspicious after all," he said, and gave the bottle back to the old man.

Since he couldn't set himself against an officer, Jisama couldn't do anything but go home and drink up the little sake that remained at the bottom of the bottle.

昔

Again he worked hard and saved money, and at last when he had saved enough, he decided to go to the wine shop. With the empty bottle in his hand and some coins in his pocket he went to the shop in the neighboring town. "Good morning," he said to the officer as he crossed the bridge in the morning. A grunt was the officer's only response. And again he had his bottle filled with sake and headed home.

As he crossed the bridge he politely said, "Thank you for doing your job, officer."

"Mister, you are not at all suspicious. I know very well you are a resident of this town. But the contents of that bottle seem suspicious. Give it to me, I will examine it," said the officer.

If I say this is sake, he will drink it all up, thought Jisama. Aloud he said, "There is just some pee in this bottle."

"Oh really. Well, I'll examine it to see if it's really pee or not. Give it to me," said the officer, and with that he snatched the bottle by force out of the old man's hands, opened the lid, and drank the sake almost all up. "It was very good pee," he said, and returned the bottle to Jisama.

Since he was helpless before an officer, he could do nothing but go home with tears in his eyes. At home he drank up the little bit of sake left at the bottom.

昔

He worked diligently again and saved money. With an empty bottle in his hand and some money in his pocket, he set off to the neighboring town. As he crossed the bridge he said good morning to the officer, getting a grunt in reply.

Jisama arrived in front of the wine shop in the neighboring town, but there he did some thinking. "Even if I say that it's pee, he will drink it up anyway. So ..." He went into the alley behind the wine shop, gathered up his clothes, and filled the bottle himself. He started home with the bottle in his hands.

Again, "Thank you for doing your job, officer," he said as he crossed the bridge.

Again the officer stopped him and said, "Mister, you are not at all suspicious. I know very well that you are a resident of this town. But the contents of that bottle seem suspicious. Give it to me, I will examine it."

"This is just a bottle of pee," said the old man.

"Yes, you had some delicious pee the other day, too. I don't care if it's pee or not, give it to me."

"No, today it's real pee."

"I said I don't care. Now give it to me."

"But I'm telling you, it really is pee."

"I don't care."

They struggled with one another, but in the end the officer forced the bottle out of Jisama's hands. He removed the lid, took one gulp, but spit it out again. Without saying a word he gave back the bottle to the old man.

And from that day on, the bridge officer never asked to examine the contents of the bottle when Jisama went to buy sake.

Oshimai

昔

COMMENT FROM MRS. FUJITA: I don't know if there were such bridge officers in fact. But it seems likely, doesn't it? I can guess in any times there are government officers who get a rake off from the people. I want to give back a humorous story like this to the government officer who makes undue profits.

Usually children like stories about something from the lower body, farts or pee and so on. As I also like those, I tell this kind of story often. You can make those stories dirty or not, it depends on the way you tell them. I think I am telling these elegantly, but what do you think?

NOTE FROM FRAN: In Japanese schools, libraries, and community centers, I often saw audiences of men and women, adults and children, enjoy Mrs. Fujita's earthy country tales together. But Americans are often skittish about hearing such tales in mixed company.

Horse Dengaku

Once upon a time, on a very hot summer day, many farmers were busy weeding in their rice fields. The mid-summer weeding was the hardest job. The rice plants were about two feet tall, so when the farmers bent down to pull weeds, the tips of the rice plants pricked their faces. It made their sweaty faces itch and sting. It even pricked their eyes sometimes. Such a hard job it was.

That day, as the farmers were all busy working, weeding their own rice fields, a low-ranking official came strolling along the narrow path between rice fields. He was walking a horse.

The official walked *tekkora, tekkora.*

The horse went *pokkora, pokkora.*

On the back of the horse was a package of miso that he was delivering to the castle.

It was such a hot day. He walked leisurely, tekkora, tekkora.

49

The horse went pokkora, pokkora. Then they passed under a big tree.

"Oh, how cool it is here under the tree! Hmm. If I bring the miso to the castle in a hurry, they won't give me credit for my speed. They will just give me more work to do. Very well, I will take a rest here."

He tied the horse's bridle to the tree, sat down, and started taking a nap. He felt no guilt for those farmers working hard in the sun. He slept under the tree. A cool breeze blew, and he felt so good. He took a nap for about half an hour. Then he woke up, yawning.

"Ahhh, ahhh. Well, I should go. They will scold me if I don't bring the miso soon."

He was going to untie the bridle. But there was no bridle. In fact, the horse was gone, too.

Now he was in a panic. He yelled at those farmers. "Hey, you! This is no time for happy weeding! My horse is gone! Go look for it! You—go that way! You—go this way! You—that way! And you—this way!"

He himself paced back and forth under the shady tree.

昔

A Jisama was weeding his rice field in the distance. He saw what was going on. He told his family, "Go to the far end of the field and weed there. When the official comes to me, pretend that you can't hear us. I'll take care of him."

Jisama went back and forth in the narrow row, weeding leisurely. The official ran to him and shouted, "Hey, farmer!"

Jisama did not reply.

"Hey, farmer!"

"Hum? Me?"

"Yes, have you seen my horse?"

"Hum?"

"Have you seen a horse with miso?"

"Ah, hum?"

"You fool, I'm asking you whether you have seen a horse with miso."

"A horse with miso? A horse with miso ... I have lived long, have seen *Konnyaku* with Miso, Daikon Radish with Miso. That kind of food is called Dengaku. They are all very good, I know. But I have never had Horse with Miso. Yes, I would very much like to try Horse Dengaku. When I go to heaven, I can tell everyone about it."

The official was very irritated. "I have no time to waste on this stupid Jisama," he said, and left.

On the other hand, Jisama said. "Good. I have no time to waste on such a stupid official. He wouldn't let us finish weeding today."

And his family continued working hard.

Oshimai

A Love Potion and a Pharmacist's Wife

Once upon a time, there was a pharmacy. They had all kinds of drugs in the store. In front of each drug, they hung a sign explaining what each drug is good for.

They had powdered charred newt. Its sign said, "Love potion. Sprinkle the powder over somebody you love. Then that person will fall in love with you. It is guaranteed."

A man came to the store and asked the pharmacist, "Does this charred newt really work?"

The pharmacist answered, "Yes, it does. Please try it on a woman. She will instantly fall in love with you."

"OK. I will try it."

He paid money and on the spot, opened the bag, and sprinkled some over the pharmacist's wife.

Instantly, she blushed at the man and blinked her eyes. Then she left her husband and followed the man.

昔

One day passed, and two days passed. But she didn't return. The pharmacist waited and waited, worried about her so much. Then one day, she came home suddenly.

"Oh, where have you been?" asked the pharmacist.

"I was living with that man," answered his wife.

"Why did you do such a thing? You have a husband here!"

"But we are selling that medicine and we guarantee it works. I had no choice but pretend to love him, didn't I?" protested the wife.

Oshimai

A Greedy Pharmacist

Once upon a time, there was a very greedy pharmacist. He wanted to make money in any way. He charred a newt, powdered it, bagged it and sold it as a love potion.

A young man came to buy it. He asked the pharmacist,

"Does this really work?"

"Of course it does! Sprinkle this, and anyone will fall in love with you."

"Really? Then I will get it."

The young man paid a lot of money, and the pharmacist handed the bag to him. Then, the pharmacist opened the bag in the man's hand and said, "Open this bag like this, and see? This is the charred newt."

Suddenly, the bag slipped out of his hand and the pharmacist got the powder all over him. The pharmacist blinked his eyes and snuggled up to the man. "I'm in love with you."

The young man was at a loss. "You're not the person I wanted to love me!"

He started running. He ran and ran, but the pharmacist kept chasing him.

"Oh, what shall I do?" the young man moaned.

Then the pharmacist said, "Once you fall in love with someone, you can't easily undo it. But there is a potion that does that. It is expensive, about ten times more expensive than the love potion. Do you want to buy it?"

"Well, if only I could get rid of you!"

The young man paid ten times as much money and bought the undo-potion. He sprinkled it over the pharmacist, and they each went back home.

Oshimai

Offering Paid Back Double

Once upon a time, there was a very cunning man. He was thinking, "I want to make easy money."

He said to some villagers, "The offertory chest in that shrine is so miraculous. Toss one *Mon* (a small coin) into the offertory chest and pray, and you will receive two Mon the next day. Why don't you try?"

He repeated this here and there around town. One of the villagers was quite greedy.

"Well, if I offer one Mon and get two Mon back the next day, that's not bad at all."

He went to the shrine, tossed one Mon into the offertory chest and prayed.

The cunning man was watching him secretly. Early the next morning, he put a second Mon in the chest.

When the greedy villager found it, he was amazed. "Wow, this is truly miraculous. I offered one Mon and received two Mon in return. Well, well ... What will happen if I offer two Mon?"

He tossed two Mon into the chest. The next day, he found four Mon in the chest.

"This is truly miraculous."

He offered all the money he had. And he told about it to the people around him. So they all tossed their money into the chest, too.

"I can hardly wait till tomorrow morning."

Saying so, they went home.

But when they went to see it the next morning, the chest was gone.

Oshimai

A Horse That Dropped Gold

Once upon a time, there was a very crafty man. He wanted to make big money. So with all his money, he bought a horse from a horse trader. It was a beautiful chestnut horse. He shoved a *Koban* (ancient gold coin) under its tail and brought it to a *Choja-sama* (rich man).

"Choja-sama, Choja-sama, this is a wonderful horse. It drops gold. Though there are many horses in this world, this is the only horse that drops gold. Trust me, you are not wasting your money. You had better buy this horse."

But Choja-sama was suspicious. "There is no horse that drops gold."

But then, the horse started doing his business.

"Choja-sama, Choja-sama, please check it."

Choja-sama picked up a stick and poked around the droppings with it. And he found a Koban.

"Wow! This really is a horse that drops gold. Yes, I'll buy this horse."

Choja-sama paid a lot of money to the man and bought the horse.

Three days, five days, and seven days went by. But gold

never came out. Choja-sama called for the man and said, "You told me a lie. This horse never drops gold."

"Choja-sama, what are you feeding this horse?" asked the man.

"I give him millet, sometimes beans, and sometimes grass. He never gets hungry. I'm feeding him many kind of things every day," answered Choja-sama.

Then, the man said, "See? Choja-sama, he will never drop gold if you are feeding such things. You have to feed him gold every day. I promise you, he will drop just as much gold as you feed him."

Oshimai

Moratorium Order

It is said that once upon a time, the government used to issue moratorium orders that cancelled all debts. Borrowed things did not have to be returned.

There was an innkeeper who was very greedy. He heard a rumor that the government might issue a moratorium order again the next day.

That night, he said to a guest in his inn, "Sir, I don't recommend that you keep your wallet in your room. Somebody might steal it. Here is a big box that I can lock up securely. Why don't you put your wallet in here?"

He got a wallet from that guest and put it into the box. Another guest said, "Yes, even if I keep my wallet under my futon, it might be stolen. I heard there are thieves pretending to be travelers. It would be much safer if you keep it for me."

Travelers carrying a lot of money all entrusted it to the innkeeper. And the innkeeper gave each of them a signed receipt which said, "I have your wallet that contains so and so money."

昔

The rumor was right. The next day, a moratorium order was issued. The innkeeper said to the guests, "I'm sorry to say this, but I have to obey what the officials say. When the moratorium order is issued, borrowed things belong to the borrowers. It means the wallets I'm keeping for you are now mine. Thank you."

The guests couldn't do anything but complain.

But one clever guest got an idea. He said, "That's all right. You had my wallet, and I admit it's yours now. But we guests were borrowing this building. Borrowed things belong to the borrowers, so, I'm sorry to say this, but you have to leave. Oh, by the way, that box belongs to this building so you have to leave it here, too. Now, please go away. This building is ours now."

The innkeeper bowed his head deeply and gave them back their money.

Oshimai

FOXES

In Japanese folktales, *Kitsune* (Fox) is a trickster and a shape-changer. When foxes lose their concentration, they are unable to maintain the illusion. The first part to regain its natural form is usually the tail. But it seems to be a rule that, when their true characters are found out, they can't stay any longer. They have to leave even if they are begged to stay.

Foxes can transform not only themselves, but also the scene around them. They can make leaves look like money, and make stones look like fish. They especially like to trick selfish people.

The stories don't always say who was behind the supernatural vision. But knowing about Fox, you can figure it out.

Tofu Seller and Fox

Once upon a time, there was a Jisama. He sold tofu, carrying the buckets suspended from a shoulder pole. In the front bucket he had fresh tofu, and in the back, fried tofu sheets and fried balls of tofu. He walked around selling them.

One day, a man came saying he had a message from a priest at a mountain temple.

"Please bring a lot of fried tofu sheets and fried balls of tofu to the temple tomorrow."

So the next day, he filled the front bucket with fried tofu sheets, and the back bucket with fried balls of tofu. And he went to the temple in the mountains.

The priest seemed very happy. "Oh, thank you. Thank you very much. I'm having many guests tomorrow, and I wanted a lot of fried tofu sheets and fried balls of tofu. I'm glad you carried them all the way up here. Please take a rest before you go."

The priest offered him good food. He even offered him sake.

"This is not sake. This is *Hannya-to*." (In Buddhism, Hannya means wisdom. To means hot water. Priests used to call sake "hot water of wisdom.") Saying so, the priest offered Jisama sake.

Jisama became happier and happier. Then he said, "Now, I have to go home. Basama is waiting."

The priest said, "Jisama, Jisama, I'm very thankful. Here in the temple, this is the best I can do for you. But you know there is a small shrine on your way back to your village. If you turn there, there is a small hot-spring inn. Take a hot bath there, stay overnight and relax. It's on me."

The priest gave him some money. Jisama walked happily, teetering a little.

"Well, should I go back to Basama right away? But I have a fat purse, so maybe I'll just stop over."

He turned at the small shrine, and saw a small inn. The landlady came out.

She was such a beautiful woman. She said, "Welcome, Jisama. Our hot spring bath is nice and warm. Do you want to take a bath, or do you want to eat first?"

"I have had plenty at the temple and I'm full. I'll take a bath first." He went to the bathing room.

The landlady said, "Please relax in the warm water. I'll come and wash your back later."

Jisama soaked in the tub, feeling so good. "When she comes, she will wash my back. I will just enjoy this warm water and wait."

He was sitting in the tub. But the landlady didn't come. "She is busy. I just have to wait a little longer."

He kept sitting in the tub. He was feeling warmer and warmer. "I have to wait till she comes to wash my back."

He waited and waited. But she didn't come.

After a while, he heard many voices. "What is that?"

He listened and heard villagers calling, "Jisama, Jisama!"

"Why, they are calling me."

So, he yelled, "Hey! I'm right here! I'm taking a bath!"

Villagers all came to him. "Jisama, what are you doing in the night-soil reservoir?"

They pulled him out.

For many days to come, Jisama was very stinky. And all the money he had in his jacket had turned back into leaves.

Oshimai

Aramaki Salmon

INSIGHT: *Aramaki-jake* is salmon preserved
with salt. Hanging from a rope through
its gills, its mouth is stuffed with salt. It is
popular as a New Year offering or gift.

One New Year's Eve, a man went into town to buy an Aramaki
salmon so that his family could celebrate the New Year.
He didn't have enough money to buy a big salmon. He shopped
around for a while, and finally picked one.

"Well, this salmon is small. But it's a whole fish. It has its
head and tail. It's good to offer to the god of the New Year. Then
my family and I will eat it."

On his way home, carrying that salmon, he saw a beautiful
young woman sobbing under a big tree by a graveyard.

"What's the matter? Why are you crying?" asked the man.

Sobbing, the woman explained, "I was scolded by my
mother-in-law."

"Why did she scold you?" asked the man.

"She sent me to town to buy an Aramaki salmon. We have
a big family, so I thought the size is most important. I bought this
salmon and came home. But my mother-in-law said, 'What good is
it without its head? You can't offer it to the god of the New Year.'
I have to go back to town and exchange it. But if I go down to
town now, I'm afraid it will be midnight before I get home. I'm so

61

scared. And that's why I'm crying."

He looked at her fish. It was huge, but had no head. "Wow, that's a big salmon," he thought.

Pretending that he was speaking from kindness, he said to the woman, "Oh lady, a young woman like you, going to town at this hour? It's dangerous. You are right. It will be very dark when you get home. No, you don't have to go. Here, I have a salmon. It's a little bit smaller than yours, but it has its head and tail. Your mother-in-law can't complain of it. I'll take yours, though it has no head. Why don't you take my salmon home?"

The woman was happy. "Are you sure we can exchange these fish? Oh, thank you. You are so kind. Thank you. Thank you very much." She thanked him many, many times, and headed home smiling happily.

The man was smiling, too. "That was good. I got this big salmon. I don't mind that it has no head. What's important is how much you can eat after you have offered it to the god of New Year. This salmon is big enough to fill up all my family. I'm so happy."

He carried it on his back and started walking home. But it was so big that it was quite heavy.

First, he was carrying the salmon by holding its rope over his shoulder. But soon he had to put his other hand around behind and support it from the bottom.

Gasping for breath, he tottered home. "I'm back!" He called at the door.

His wife came to the door and asked, "Why, what are you carrying on your back?"

The man said, "Of course, it's an Aramaki salmon."

He put it down. It was a big gravestone.

Oshimai

Samurai and Jisama

Once upon a time, there was a Jisama who went to a party. He got a little drunk, and was given an Aramaki salmon to take home. Carrying it on his back, he was walking.

He saw a Samurai warrior coming from the opposite direction.

"A Samurai is coming. I had better make way for him."

He stepped aside, but the Samurai moved to the same side. "Oh, no."

Jisama moved to the other side. So did the Samurai. Jisama moved back. So did the Samurai. Jisama moved back again. So did the Samurai again. Again, and again, and again and again.

Jisama could avoid the Samurai no more. He bumped into him and fell on his back.

"Oh, no! He might put me to the sword!" In those days, Samurai were allowed to kill on the spot.

Jisama apologized and bowed his head down.

But when he opened his eyes, there was no Samurai.

And his Aramaki salmon was gone, too.

Oshimai

A Fox Apprentice

Once upon a time, a little boy visited a priest in a temple. "I would like to learn the teachings of Buddha. Please take me as your apprentice."

From then on, this apprentice worked hard in the temple. Reading a sutra, cleaning the temple, everything he did, he did well. From early morning till late at night, he worked hard. He was a favorite with his master.

昔

One day, this apprentice was hand-copying a sutra. While he copied, maybe it was because he started the day too early, he became drowsy. With his face on the desk, he fell asleep.

It is said that in sleep, people reveal their true characters. This apprentice revealed his tail. And the priest saw it.

The priest said, "No matter who you are, it's all right to practice Buddhism. Even if you are a fox."

But the fox said, "No. Now that you know who I am, I cannot stay here any longer. But you have been so nice to me. I would like to do you a favor. Tomorrow evening, when the sun sets, please go out to the back yard and look to the west."

Saying so, this apprentice left the temple.

昔

Next day, the priest went out to the back yard and waited for sunset. When the sun was setting, the sky beyond turned purple. There appeared many saints, like *Shakyamuni*, *Amitabha*, and *Bhechadjaguru*, each surrounded with beams of light.

It was such a glorious sight.

When the priest put his hands together for prayer, they disappeared.

That was what the fox did to show his gratitude to the priest.

Oshimai

Old Man and Grateful Fox

Once upon a time, there was an old man, Jisama. One day, he went to a mountain to gather firewood. There, he found a fox with its foot caught in a snare. Jisama freed the fox.

The fox was very thankful. "I would like to repay you somehow, but I have no money. I have nothing to give you. But I have power to make a vision. If you have something you want to see, I will show you that. Do you want to see *Amano Hashidate* (a famous beautiful sightseeing spot)? Or do you want to see *Matsushima* (another famous sightseeing spot)?"

But Jisama replied, "No, I don't want to see such places. If you really can show me something, I want to see where my son was killed. My son was conscripted for war the other day, and villagers say he was killed. But his body never came back. I feel he is still alive. I can't believe he is dead. How did it happen? I want to see how he died."

The fox nodded and started chanting something very softly. Then, the area got light, and Jisama heard battle cries. He was right in the middle of battle. Soldiers on both sides were fighting each

65

other fiercely. Astonished, Jisama stared at them. Then he shouted, "Oh, the one over there! That's my son!"

At the same time, Jisama saw an arrow fly toward his son and pierce his arm. And his son collapsed there. "Oh, no! My son died from the arrow wound."

Jisama kept watching. Soldiers on their side were winning. They chased after the enemy, leaving behind the dead and wounded. Some had been shot by an arrow, some by a bullet. As Jisama kept looking, his son stood up and staggered into the woods.

"Oh, my son is alive!"

Then, the vision was gone.

"I see! After the war, the dead soldiers were carried home on stretchers. The wounded ones came home leaning on some-one's shoulder. But my son's body never returned. That's because he hid in the woods."

昔

Jisama didn't know where that wood was. But he went here and there and looked for it. Finally, he found the wood that the fox had showed him. Calling his son's name, he searched through the wood.

His son was hiding in a cave. His wound from the arrow was healing. He was living on mice and nuts in the wood.

Jisama wanted to take him home right away. But people were saying that there would be another battle soon. If Jisama took him home, his son would be taken for war again.

"Stay here for a while until you become fully well."

Jisama left him and returned with food and clothes.

I don't know any more of this story. But I think when the war ended, they lived happily ever after.

Oshimai

Homesick Bride and Helpful Fox

A young bride came from a village three mountains away. Her new mother-in-law turned out to be a very mean woman. Usually mothers-in-law were kind enough to send their daughters-in-law back home once in a while, making the excuse to do some errands. But this mean mother-in-law never sent the young wife back home. She kept saying, "Oh, we are so busy," and ordered her to carry rice plants to the field, then to plant them, then to weed the field.

So, this young wife had not seen her mother since her marriage. She would often go to the mountain behind the house and weep. "I miss my mother! I miss my mother!"

Once, she even asked her mother-in-law if she could visit her mother. But the mean mother-in-law just replied, "If your mother were sick and dying, I would send you back home. But if there is no good reason, a wife should not visit her mother. Do you understand?"

This poor young wife had nothing more to say. She just missed her mother every day.

Once when she was crying on the mountain behind their house, she saw a fox watching her.

After a few days, a man came from her home village. He said to the mother-in-law, "The mother of your daughter-in-law is sick and dying. She is begging to see her daughter. I was sent here to tell you."

"Oh, that's terrible. Now, hurry," the mother-in-law told the young wife. "You must go and see your mother." Finally she was sent back home.

She was so worried. Her only wish was that she could see her mother again before she died. She ran and ran and ran, over the three mountains. She was all out of breath when she returned to her childhood home.

There she saw her lively mother dashing toward her. "What happened? Why are you back now? Did your mother-in-law kick you out? Have you done something to offend her?" her mother asked.

"No, mother. I was told you were sick and dying. I came running all the way to see you. So you are not sick?" the daughter asked.

"No, not at all!" the mother replied.

The daughter explained that a man living near there had come and called her. So they went to ask him. But the man said, "I have been home for a couple of days now. I did not go to your village."

"Then, it might be …" the daughter hit upon a strange idea but she did not say anything.

After all, since she was already there, her mother said she should stay and relax.

After three or four days, she went back to her new home.

She told her mother-in-law, "My mother is all right now. I don't know why, maybe it's because she could see me."

The next day, the young wife went to the mountain behind the house again.

Behind the tree, as she had supposed, there was the fox watching her.

After that, the bride saved choice bits from her meal and

brought them to the mountain.

    Oshimai

昔

COMMENT FROM MRS. FUJITA: Usually it's men who are deceived by the shape-changing fox. But in this story it is a woman (mother-in-law) who is fooled. That is very rare in these folktales. Maybe it is because women did not go out very often in the old days.

From: "Prince Hanzoku terrorised by a nine-tailed fox"
By Utagawa Kuniyoshi

ONI

What is *Oni?* When people die, we say, "That person has become a member of the Oni." So Oni are the spirits of the dead. I heard that in China, the calligraphy character Oni means the spirit of the dead. In another book, I have read that Oni represent invisible forces of nature.

The northeast (Ox and Tiger) direction is called Gate of Oni. Oni are said to live in that direction and that is the reason why Oni have the horns of an ox and wear a tiger skin loincloth.

I find in books many different explanations about Oni, but I personally believe the explanation I heard from the farmer next door when I was a child. According to him, Oni is a force of nature. It creates mountains and rivers, but it is also ruthless and destroys them of its own will. It is the cause of every disaster, like typhoon, flood and epidemic. You can see why people in the old days wished to send Oni away.

Enma-samma, the guardian of heaven and hell, is the boss of Oni. He sends them to bring souls for judgment. They know the date you will die! There is an old Japanese saying, "When you talk about next year, Oni laugh at you." It means you can't be sure what you will do in the far future.

In With Oni

Once upon a time, there lived a very poor man. He was so poor that he often didn't have enough to eat. One year on *Setsubun* day (the day before the first day of spring), he said to himself, "Today is Setsubun day. I have to scatter roasted soybeans." He called out to his wife, "Hey, would you bring some roasted soybeans?"

But his wife replied, "We have none. Though we are saving some soybeans for planting."

"Oh, are those all we have? If we roast them, we'll have nothing to plant this spring. But we can't do without soybeans at Setsubun. All right, all right," he told his wife, "bring a handful of them!"

He prepared the roasting pot. He started to roast the soybeans, stirring *kara koro, kara koro.*

"I have got soybeans. I will snip a holly branch outside and get a bamboo strainer from my kitchen. But what about a sardine head? I wouldn't dare to go to a fish market and ask for just the head of a sardine. What shall I do?" he thought while he stirred and roasted the soybeans.

> Kara koro, kara koro, kara koro, kara koro.
> (sound of stirring)

It is very important to roast the soybeans thoroughly. Scattering them is a message to Oni that you wish them not to come back until these beans sprout. So you have to make sure those soybeans will never sprout. Also, with a sardine head, you are requesting Oni not to come back till this sardine head starts swimming. I'm sure a sardine head doesn't swim.

Oni attach importance to eyes. There are Oni with one eye, two eyes, and three eyes. Three-eyes Oni is so proud of himself, saying "I have as many as three eyes!" But we are a little smarter than they are. We show our bamboo strainer, full of holes that look like thousands of eyes. Knowing that people use this thing with thousands of eyes every day, Oni get scared and run away. But there are some who dare to enter our house. Then we can poke Oni's eyes with prickly holly leaves and send them away.

Kara koro, kara koro, kara koro, kara koro.

He roasted the beans, thinking this and that. "Beans are about ready now. I only have to wait for night to come."

It grew darker and darker, and from neighbors' houses he could hear people chant, "*ONI wa soto, fuKU wa uchi.*" (Out with Oni, in with good luck.)

He thought, "I'll scatter my beans, too."

Then a strange idea came upon him. "I have done this every year, chanting 'Out with Oni, in with good luck.' But good luck never came in here, even a tiny bit of it. So, this year, I would like to try doing it differently. How about chanting '*ONI wa uchi* (in with Oni)'?"

He started to yell, "In with Oni, in with Oni!"

By that time, many, many Oni had been sent away from neighboring houses.

They started to head for his house, *zoro zoro, zoro zoro.* (sound of footsteps)

There were Red Oni, Black Oni and Blue Oni. There were huge ones and small ones. There were old ones and child ones.

72

Zoro zoro, zoro zoro. Soon his small house was filled with many Oni. They sat around the hearth in the center of the room, and warmed themselves.

The biggest Oni of all spoke up, "I have been an Oni for a long, long time. And this is the first time I have been invited in on Setsubun night. Oh, I'm so glad! But is this fire the only hospitality you will offer us?"

Flustered, the man said, "Oh, I'm sorry. Please have some of these." He served all the soybeans he had roasted. But it was so little, just a handful. Each Oni ate one or two beans, and it was gone.

He asked his wife, "Don't we have something else?"

His wife said, "I have one nice petticoat. I'll take it to a pawnshop."

She pawned her petticoat and came home with some sake. But a petticoat is a petticoat. Even though it was a nice one, she couldn't get a lot of sake. Each Oni had a lick, and the sake was gone.

"Don't we have something else?" The couple looked and looked in the kitchen.

The biggest Oni stood up and said, "This woman pawned her petticoat to give us a treat. It was very delicious. We have never had such a wonderful treat before."

"Never," all the rest agreed.

The biggest Oni continued, "I can't wear my tiger skin loincloth when this woman pawned her petticoat for us. Now, take my loincloth to the pawnshop. I want to give you back a treat." He took a towel, wrapped himself with it, took off his tiger skin loincloth and gave it to the woman. She ran to the pawnshop again, this time with the Oni's loincloth.

The pawnbroker was so surprised.

He said, "This is such a treasure! I couldn't take this! But if you need some money now, I will give you all the money I have. Take this strongbox full of money."

She took the money, bought sake and food, loaded them in a wagon, and pulled them home.

Now it was time for the feast. They started to drink, sing and dance.

When it comes to drinking, there is no difference between humans and Oni.

There are some who become more and more jolly. There are some who become more and more depressed. There are some who become more and more angry. They yell in a loud voice, and nobody knows what they are angry about. Some like dancing. The easiest ones to take care of are the ones who fall sleep. They eat, drink, and when their stomach is filled, they just lie down and start snoring.

Stepping over sleeping Oni, crawling under dancing Oni, and hopping this way and that way, the Oni children played *Oni-gokko*. (A game of tag. The one who is "it" is called the Oni. It is funny that Oni children play Oni-gokko like human children.)

It was, indeed, a jolly and merry mess!

昔

Suddenly, the earliest rooster cried, "*Koki ko ko!*"

Some Oni startled awake. They woke the sleeping ones up, and fetched their children. Pulling those sleepy ones and holding the small children in their arms, they hurried away.

Among the bottles and barrels, many wonderful treasures were left behind. Oni's miracle bag was there. The mallet of luck was there. Oni's iron pikes (spears), fur loincloths, and many precious things were all over the place.

The man and his wife sat in the middle of the room,

74

looking at each other.

"It was like a dream," the man said to his wife. Then he stood up and started to gather all the things the Oni had left behind.

"I must keep them safe till next Setsubun to return them to the Oni," he said.

He collected them together and stored them in the cellar.

昔

Like a miracle, everything he did that year was a great success. In spring, he went to the mountain to gather wild vegetables and came back with tender bracken and bamboo shoots, almost more than he could carry. In autumn, he came back with plenty of mushrooms. When he went hunting, he felt like pheasants were flying toward his bullet. When he set a net in the river, it was always heavy with fish. Crops in his garden were so plentiful that he always had more than enough to share with his neighbors.

Soon, he was able to get his wife's petticoat and Oni's loincloth back from the pawnshop.

昔

The next Setsubun came. The couple had put new tatami-mats in the parlor, shined the door, and got new paper on their shoji screens. They set the table and prepared a feast, and put all the Onis' treasures on a wooden offering table. They waited for night.

It grew darker and darker, and they could hear the chant, "Out with Oni, out with Oni," coming from this neighbor and that neighbor.

"Good, it's about the time," they thought and in a big voice, the man started yelling, "In with Oni! In with Oni!"

But nobody came in.

"In with Oni!" he repeated.

"This is strange. Last year, there were so many. Where have they gone?" He slid open the door and tried to see through the darkness.

There they were! By the front gate, by the fence, by the bush, he saw many faces he remembered from last year.

"There you are! Please come in. This year, we can offer you treats without running to the pawnshop. They are all ready. Now, please come in!" the man said to the Oni.

But the Oni didn't come in. They just grinned at each other.

"Oh, please come in. I have your things set on a table. You must come in and get them," he said.

The biggest Oni stepped forward and said, "This year, we can't come in."

"Why? I enjoyed it so much last year. I wanted to thank you. I prepared sake and many, many dishes for you. Please come in and have some," he begged.

"No, we can't," Oni insisted.

"Why? I can't accept that until I know why. Tell me why," he said.

Then that Oni started to explain. "Last year, we had the best time ever since we had become Oni. Sake was so delicious. It was so much fun that we forgot the time. Then the rooster crowed and it was morning. We hurried to our Oni Island. We barely got in a second before the gate closed. But we forgot our bags. We forgot our mallets of luck, spiked clubs, and even loincloths. Enma-sama, the ruler of our world, was so angry. He asked us what we were going to do about the things we had left. We said, 'We will go back there on next Setsubun and get them.' But Enma-sama said, 'What are you talking about? When you talk about next year, you don't know anything. Those are precious treasures. You don't believe that man will give you back those treasures, do you? See, all the Oni here are laughing at you because you are talking about next year.' So we had to make ourselves small for a year. It has been a long year, hasn't it?" this Oni said and looked back at his people.

The other Oni nodded.

"So, we can't come in this year," this Oni said.

The man understood and said, "I see. I understand why, and I won't ask you anymore. But I want you to take all the things I prepared." He gave them barrels of sake. He wrapped the snacks in straw wrappers and gave them to the Oni.

He gave back all the things they had forgotten last year, too.

Then the biggest Oni took out one small bag and said, "You don't have enough muscles to handle our other treasures. But I think you can use this bag."

Oni handed it to the man. That bag was a magic bag. The money inside would never decrease, no matter how often he removed some.

That man became very wealthy.

I don't know how many generations have passed. But still, on Setsubun day, his descendants prepare sake and food by their house gate. And they chant, "In with Oni, in with Oni."

Oshimai

昔

COMMENT FROM MRS. FUJITA: This is a story I learned from Toshiko Endo. It is a long story, so sometimes I omit details like the explanation of the roasted soybeans and the sardine head.

NOTE FROM FRAN: On my family's first visit to Japan in 1975, we attended a Setsubun celebration at a temple. The priests tossed packets of roasted soybeans to the crowd. I think we were supposed to throw the beans into the corners of our house, to drive out the Oni. But we were staying at a hotel, so we just ate the beans, a few at a time. We were already fond of "soy nuts"! But we had learned the hard way that you can't eat too many at once, because, like other beans, they can cause digestive mischief.

Setsubun

> **INSIGHT:** Country folklore blamed many mala-
> dies on "worms" in the stomach. When the
> stomach rumbles with hunger, your worms
> are crying. When your stomach seethes with
> anger, your worms are stirring around. When
> you have a stomach ache, your worms are
> fighting.

Once upon a time, there was Jisama and Basama. One day Jisama held his stomach and said, "Basama, Basama, I have a very bad stomach ache. What's the matter with me?"

And Basama, rubbing his stomach, said "Jisama, Jisama, maybe some worms in your stomach are fighting."

Jisama said, "Worms in my stomach are fighting? Well, what should I do?"

And Basama said, "I don't know, go to the priest of the temple and ask him."

So Jisama went to the temple holding his hurting stomach and said, "Oh priest, some worms in my stomach seem to be fighting, so I have a severe stomach ache. What should I do? How can I get rid of fighting worms?"

The priest was busy, so perhaps he didn't listen very well. He said, "Oh, you have some trouble with worms? Well, something that gets rid of worms is a frog. You need a frog."

So Jisama went to the rice field, caught a frog and swallowed it into his stomach.

The frog got rid of the worms and his stomach ache was gone.

昔

But next the frog went around this way *petakuta petakuta* (sound of hopping) and that way petakuta petakuta in his stomach. He felt very sick. Jisama asked Basama, "My stomach ache has gone, but now a frog hops around petkuta petakuta in my stomach and I'm feeling very sick."

And Basama said, "I don't know what to do. Go to the temple and ask."

So Jisama went to the temple again and said, "Priest, Priest, the worms stopped fighting, but now a frog hops around petkuta petakuta, so I'm feeling very bad. What should I do?"

And the priest said, "Well, a frog? For getting rid of a frog you just need a snake."

Jisama was convinced, went to the field, caught a snake and put it into his stomach.

The snake got rid of the frog, and petakuta petakuta was gone.

But now the snake slithered around, *zuru zuru, nyoro nyoro, zuru zuru nyoro nyoro*. (slithering sound) The man felt very sick.

昔

"Basama Basama, the frog's petkuta petakuta has gone, but now a snake goes zuru zuru nyoro nyoro. What should I do?" said Jisama.

And Basama said, "A snake? I don't know, go to the temple

79

and ask."

He went back to the temple and asked, "Priest, Priest, petakuro petakuro has gone but now a snake goes zuru zuru nyoro nyoro. I'm feeling sick. What should I do?"

The priest said, "A snake? If you have trouble with a snake, you have to get rid of it with a pheasant."

Jisama thought that must be right, so he went to the mountains, caught a pheasant and put it into his stomach.

That pheasant got rid of the snake and zuru zuru nyoro nyoro was gone.

But now the pheasant fluttered its wings, *batakuta batakuta*.

昔

"Basama, Basama, zuru zuru nyoro nyoro has gone, but now the pheasant flutters batakuta batakuta. What should I do?"

Basama said, "A pheasant fluttering? I don't know. Go to the temple and ask."

Jisama went to the temple again, and said, "Priest, Priest, zuru zuru nyoro nyoro has gone, but now a pheasant flutters batakuta batakuta. What should I do?"

And the priest said, "A pheasant? To get rid of a pheasant you need a hunter."

Jisama thought that was just right. He went to the mountain, found a hunter who was going to shoot a bird, caught him and put him into his stomach. The hunter got rid of the pheasant, so batakuta batakuta stopped.

But the butt of the hunter's gun poked his stomach here and there, *zuburi zuburi*, and gave him a lot of pain.

昔

"Basama, Basama, fluttering batajkutaa batakuta of the pheasant is gone, but the hunter's gun, zuburi zuburi, hurts my stomach. What shall I do?"

80

Basama said, "The hunter's gun sticks you, zuburi zuburi? I don't know what you should do. Go to the temple and ask the priest."

And Jisama did so, and said, "Priest, Priest! Batakura batakura is gone but this time the hunter's gun sticks me, zuburi zuburi, and I can't stand much more of this. What can I do?"

And the priest said, "A hunter? Something to get rid of a hunter is ... Well we can't find it easily around here ... It's an Oni. An Oni can get rid of a hunter."

Jisama thought, "That sounds just right. There are no Oni around here, so I'll go to *Onigashima* (Oni Island). But an Oni may eat me up if I fail to catch him."

So he got close to an Oni slowly, caught him from behind quickly and put him into his stomach.

And the Oni got rid of the hunter and Jisama had no more trouble with zuburi zuburi.

But now the Oni's horn poked his stomach here and there, *chikun chikun.*

昔

"Basama, Basama! A hunter's gun sticking me, zuburi zuburi, has gone, but now an Oni's horn pokes my stomach and I can't stand it. What shall I do?"

Basama said again, "An Oni's horn is poking your stomach, I don't know. Go to the temple and ask."

Then Jisama went to the temple and asked, "Priest, Priest! A hunter's gun sticking me, zuburi zuburi, has gone but now an Oni's horn is poking me, chikun chikun, and I have a lot of pain."

"An Oni? If it's an Oni, we can get rid of it. Here are some roasted soybeans left over from Setsubun."

Jisama swallowed the toasted soybeans, saying "*ONI wa soto, fuKU wa uchi.*"

This caught the Oni by surprise.

You know, it was dark inside the stomach, and in the dark some beans sprinkled down, *para para para para*. As the Oni ran around in the stomach, *uro uro, uro uro*, searching for a way to escape from those beans, he saw a small light down below.

He thought this way should be an exit, and he ran away to that direction to get out.

In fact that small light was the hole of Jisama's bottom and the Oni flew out of there,

> *SettsuBUUN!*

> *Oshimai*

昔

COMMENT FROM MRS. FUJITA: Such a story can't exist in reality, with Jisama putting a frog, snake, and at last an Oni into his stomach. But by declaring "he put it into his stomach" a teller makes the listener believe. If such a story was illustrated in a picture book or performed in a puppet show, it would be too concrete. In their heads the listeners may question, "Is it really possible?" But if they enjoy listening to this story, you can say that your telling has succeeded.

TIP FROM FRAN: At the last part of this story, say in a small voice "Settsu –" drawing it out; then say "–BUUN!" to show the comfortable feeling when the Oni was blown far away.

Danjuro Enma

INSIGHT: *Kabuki* is classical Japanese dance-drama featuring stylized costumes and elaborate makeup, in which all the actors are men.

Once upon a time, there was a great Kabuki actor called Danjuro. He always performed his part very well. When he was playing a Samurai, he was a cool warrior, drawing his sword on the enemy in style. When he was playing a lady, he walked gracefully in a beautiful kimono. When he was playing an old beggar woman, he looked so ugly and miserable ... and you should see how feebly he could totter! Whatever role he played, he could play it exquisitely.

Without warning, this Danjuro died suddenly. His corpse was dressed in a white funeral kimono. Red Oni and Blue Oni brought his spirit to see Enma-sama, the lord of the underworld. There were a lot of people waiting in line in front of Enma-sama. One by one, Enma-sama was deciding if that person should go up to heaven or down to hell.

Enma-sama always asks these three questions: "Did you do the world good while you were alive? Did you have children? Were you good to your parents?"

If the answers to these three are "Yes," Enma-sama will probably say, "To Heaven!"

It is no use lying to Enma-sama. He has a mirror called

Jo-hari. He can see in the mirror everything that person did while living. "Oh, you were good to your parents. You had many children, too. You worked hard as a farmer. Good, good. You can go up to heaven." Saying things like that, he decides one by one.

昔

Now, it was Danjuro's turn. Enma-sama asked Danjuro, "Did you do the world good while you were alive? Did you have children? Were you good to your parents?"

"Yes," answered Danjuro.

Enma-sama looked into the Jo-hari mirror. He saw a scary-looking bandit robbing money from a traveler and killing him. "What? You were a bandit?"

Then, Enma-sama saw a beautiful woman in the mirror. She was cheating a man out of money. "What? You were cheating people?"

Then, Enma-sama saw an old beggar woman. Making a sad face, she was saying, "Please, Mister, pity me and give me some money."

"What kind of job is this?" asked Enma-sama.

"Those are the parts I played. I was an actor. I played many parts to entertain other people. They enjoyed my play. I did the world good," said Danjuro.

But Enma-sama didn't know what a play was.

"You say 'play' but I don't know what it is. I don't know what an actor does. So, you have to show it to me here."

Then Danjuro said, "But Enma-sama, I can't show it here. It is said that a play is eighty percent costume and twenty percent makeup. I have no costume. I have no cosmetics. I can't do it."

"I see. You need a costume. All right, you can use my Enma regalia," said Enma-sama.

"Oh, thank you. I'll borrow it and do a play of Enma-sama," said Danjuro.

Enma-sama took off his crown, sandals and clothing. He put on Danjuro's thin white funeral kimono. Trembling with the chill, he watched Danjuro put on his own under-kimono, then his kimono, then his *hakama* pleated trousers, his crown, sandals.

Then, Danjuro held Enma-sama's scepter. And he stood solemnly.

Yes, he was such a great actor. With the costume, he looked as solemn as Enma-sama. Adding to that, he had such a great voice. With that great voice, he said, "Red Oni and Blue Oni over there! Take this man to hell."

He sounded more dignified than the real Enma-sama. The real Enma-sama was trembling in the thin white funeral kimono. Red Oni and Blue Oni grabbed him from both sides. He yelled, "I'm the real Enma. I am the real one!"

But Danjuro said, "Don't let him yell. Drop him in, fast."

Danjuro sounded so dignified that Red Oni and Blue Oni believed him easily. They dropped the real Enma-sama down to hell.

Since that time, it is Danjuro sitting in the Enma chair.

And I shouldn't be saying this aloud, but Danjuro is from Fukushima. So, when you stand in front of him, you should whisper to him in Fukushima dialect, "Aren't you Danjuro?"

He might do you a favor.

Oshimai

昔

COMMENT FROM MRS. FUJITA: Where do people go when they die? The answer is different depending upon your religion. But in Japanese folktales, people first go to Enma-sama. He decides whether they go up to heaven or down to hell. In his Jo-hari mirror he can see people's actions while alive. 'Jo' means clean and clear. 'Hari' means glass and crystal.

Even if people declare to Enma-sama only their good actions, everything is shown in the clear crystal mirror. So, they can't cheat Enma-sama.

But Danjuro cheated Enma-sama. He must have been a great actor to do that.

From: "Oni depicted in Konjaku Gazu Zoku Hyakki"
By Toriyama Sekien. 1712-1788

KAPPA

Kappa (water sprite) is very strong as long as he has water in his head plate. It was believed that Kappa pulls children and horses down into the river. When he is caught doing mischief, he signs a paper or sometimes gives ointment that is good for a cut on the skin. There are some temples that worship Kappa. They offer cucumbers to Kappa. Probably Kappa was a god of water.

Kappa's Cream

Once upon a time, there was a village that had a problem. When young ladies or wives went to the outhouse, a cold hand came out of the toilet hole and stroked their bottoms. They didn't like it. Ladies didn't want to go to the outhouse any more.

An old lady, Basama, decided on a plan. She hid a knife in her kimono and went to the outhouse. She squatted there and waited. But the hand didn't come. She waited and waited.

At last the cold hand came out of the hole and stroked her bottom.

She took the knife in her right hand, grabbed the cold

hand with her left hand and cut it off.

"*Gya!!*" Something screamed and ran away.

昔

That night, somebody knocked on Basama's door. *Ton, ton.* (knock, knock)

She opened the door. Kappa came in. Holding his arm like this (hide one hand under your other arm) he said, "Basama, Basama, please give me back my hand. I'm very sorry for what I have done to your villagers. I'll never do any trick again, so please give me back my hand."

"Well, but if I give you back your hand, you'll probably start doing mischief again."

"No, no, Kappas are different from humans: we never lie. I'll never play another trick on your villagers. So please give me back my hand."

"But you see, even if I give it back, it's already cut off. It won't do you any good."

"That's not true. We have a special ointment called Kappa's Cream. It can heal anything."

"Oh, really? You have such a thing? Put it on this cut off hand, and if it works, you can have your hand."

Kappa took out a sea shell container. He scooped the cream and put some on the cut surfaces of his arm and his hand. He put them together. Soon, he could move his hand again.

Basama was very surprised.

"It's an amazing thing. Very well, your hand is yours now. From now on, never do any harm to humans. Do you agree?"

Kappa bowed deeply and said, "Thank you very much. And please keep this ointment."

昔

After that, Basama started a pharmacy. But she was given

such a small amount of ointment that, if she sold it as it was, it would be gone so quickly. So she thinned and thinned it. She sold it little by little and made a fortune.

Oshimai

昔

COMMENT FROM MRS. FUJITA: When I lived in Fukushima, my house had an old-style outhouse toilet. There was a big cave under it. Maybe because it didn't have a tight lid, or the house itself was old, the toilet was very drafty. When I squatted there, the cold wind swept up from below. It was very cold. I shivered as if the draft was a Kappa's wet hand.

Today, we have flush toilets. The seats are even equipped with heaters. There is no chance for Kappa to appear there. There is no chance for the brave Basama to take an active part, either.

Sumo Wrestling With Kappa

Once upon a time, there was a boy in a village. He was very strong.

One day, when the village boy was walking by the river, a very small boy was standing there. And when the strong boy walked past the small boy, the small boy said, "Let's wrestle Sumo style."

The village boy looked at the little boy and thought, "He can't possibly beat me." So he said, "All right, all right."

Then the two of them started sumo wrestling immediately. But the small boy was much stronger than he looked, and in a second he got the strong village boy down. Then he started pulling him into the water. The strong boy was drowned in the river.

昔

Another day, another village boy was walking by the river. This boy didn't look as strong as the last boy, but the small boy appeared and said, "Let's Sumo wrestle."

"All right, all right," replied the village boy.

The small boy tried to start the match immediately, but the village boy said, "Wait. In Sumo wrestling, manners are very important. So let's bow first."

He bowed at the small boy. And the small boy hastily bowed back.

Then they stamped their feet and put their hands on their knees.

"Ready, start!"

In a second, the small boy was defeated and he ran away into the river.

昔

The important thing is, if you meet a boy by a river and he says "Let's Sumo wrestle," that boy must be a Kappa. So you have to make him bow before you start or you will lose and will be pulled into the river. If he bows, the water in his head plate will spill out and he will lose his super power.

Oshimai

MANY GODS

In traditional Shinto belief, everything—living or not—has a spirit called *kami*. These are "small g" gods, not divine or omnipotent, but they were still important in traditional village life.

We say that there are eight million Shinto gods in Japan. So if we look around, there are gods everywhere.

The God of Age

> INSIGHT: In the old days, *Toshigami-sama* (god of age) went from house to house on New Year's Eve to distribute another year of life to each person. A baby was considered already to be one year old at birth, so he became two years old on his first New Year's Day.

There was once a forty-year-old man who said to himself, "I don't want to receive any more years from Toshigami-sama. The older I get, the more my back will be bent, the more wrinkles I will have, and the less work I will be able to do. I have to figure out some way to avoid Toshigami-sama so that I won't get any older."

"It seems that if you're inside the house Toshigami-sama will find you. It does no good to hide in the bathroom or in the closet. Maybe I can find a good hiding place outdoors."

On New Year's Eve he looked around and found a huge hole in the corner of a daikon radish field, where farmers had dug a compost pit. "This will make a great hiding place," he thought. "Toshigami-sama won't think to look in a hole. I'll hide in here until next morning, New Year's Day."

So the man jumped in the hole, crouched down and waited until New Year's Eve was over and New Year's Day came.

昔

But the god in charge of distributing the years that year was a lazy god. He came down from the land of the gods dragging a huge sack filled with wishes for abundant crops, flourishing business, and well-being of the family, as well as plenty of years to distribute. At first he worked diligently, giving years to everyone. "One for the father, one for the mother, one for each child, one for the dog, one for the cat, one for the rooster, there seems to be no grandmother but one for her, too," he said. He visited house after house to give everyone his or her year.

After a while, however, he began to get tired of it. "Oh, I don't feel like visiting the village on the other side of the river. I won't go there this year." So he thought he would turn back to his homeland in heaven, but there were still many years left in his sack. If he went home with them, his boss wouldn't be happy with him. He had to leave them somewhere.

He walked around, looking for a good place to throw the years away. If he left them on the side of a road, the grass might get old all of a sudden and wither. If he dumped them under a tree, its leaves would fall and its branches would break off.

After a while, he came to the daikon field. "Oh, here's a

nice hole! I can throw away my years in here," he said. He put the sack on the ground, turned it over, and dumped all the remaining years into the hole. "Well well, I've finished my job for this year." Satisfied, he traveled back to his land.

昔

New Year's Day dawned. As the sky was becoming light, the man thought, "Thank goodness I didn't meet Toshigami-sama," and tried to get out of the hole.

He had jumped in nimbly the evening before, but now he couldn't even straighten his bent back. "It must be because I was crouching in this cold, damp hole all night," he said, and with much difficulty he crawled out at last.

Wiping the dirt off his hands, he looked at them and found them wrinkled like crumpled paper. "What's happening to me?" he wondered, but he still didn't realize what was going on.

He went to the river to wash the dirt off his hands. He dug a small ditch in the ground on the river bank so that water from the river would flow in. He washed his hands and face in the ditch, but when the water surface became calm, he looked in and saw his reflection.

And there he was, turned into an old man of eighty!

Oshimai

昔

COMMENT FROM MRS. FUJITA: When I was a child, we used to count our age in this traditional way. We couldn't treat our year carelessly, because it was a gift from god.

After WWII, we began to count our age in American style and many families began to celebrate birthdays, so the New Year became less important. But through a story like this I want to hand down the idea that god gave us life and each year of age.

Toshigami-sama brought the years in a large bag, along with *Gokoku Hokyo* (good rice crop), *Shobai hanjyo* (brisk business) and *Kanai Anzen* (the safety of one's house).

According to my Uncle in the Field who told me this story, sometimes Toshigami-sama was careless and got a hole in the bag by snagging it on a branch of a tree. If your share of Gokoku Hokyo fell through the hole, that year you would have a very small rice crop.

He said that if Toshigami-sama lost some of the *Toshi* (year of age) through the hole and ran short of them, he wouldn't deliver one to the old woman who didn't complain in spite of her age and frailty. She wouldn't get any older!

It was great times.

NOTE FROM FRAN: Mrs. Fujita also told me how, in preparation for Toshigami-sama's visit, the house had to be cleaned top to bottom, new clothes prepared, all food cooked in advance, etc., so that the heavenly visitor would feel at home—or he might not come to your house. It may have been heaven for Toshigami-sama, but I'll bet it was hell on the housewives.

However, since she and I never have our houses perfectly clean for New Year's Eve, we trust we will not get any older.

Apologizing Crow

INSIGHT: The story of how crow got dyed
black, "Owl's Paint Shop," is in *Folktales From
the Japanese Countryside* (2007).

A long, long time ago, around the time when god had just created people and animals, a crow accidentally dyed himself all black. He didn't like it. So he went to god and begged to change the color.

But god said, "Oh, no. I can't do that. Once I set a deadline, I can't change it. But I feel sorry for you. I will make you my messenger bird. First, bring this medicine to people. The powder in this bag gives long life to people. They will live for several hundred years. Don't spill it. Make sure it gets to them. Of all the animals I created, I suppose people are the smartest. I want them to govern the world, so I want to give them long life. The medicine is in this bag. Be sure it gets to people."

The crow was very happy. He held the bag in his beak and flew off to people.

But on the way, he became tired. He stopped on a tree in the woods and stretched one wing. He mumbled, "Woo, I'm tired. I'm tired."

He stretched his other wing, and then he cawed as if he was yawning, "Kaaaa."

Then the bag fell from his beak.

A puff of wind scattered the powder all around the trees in the woods.

So that's why trees have long life. They can grow for a hundred or two hundred years.

People were supposed to live for a hundred or two hundred years. But the crow couldn't bring the medicine to them.

昔

Crow didn't have the nerve to face god, so he didn't go back to him.

What if he told the truth to people: "You were supposed to live for two hundred years"? They might kill him. So he couldn't tell people the truth.

But when people who are only in their fifties or sixties lie dying, the crow flies to their house. On the rooftop, he caws, "I'm sorry. Kaaaa. I'm sorry. Kaaaa."

The crow is apologizing.

Oshimai

昔

COMMENT FROM MRS. FUJITA: On the roof of a house where someone is dying, they say that a crow kaws differently. It sounds more like "*Gaoru!*" instead of "Kaaa." Gaoru in Fukushima dialect means "so tired that one can't stand up again." Perhaps he hopes we will excuse his carelessness.

Eighteen Years to Live

Once upon a time, there was a traveler. He had finished his business and was almost home, just one more mountain to go. But it was already dark.

"It's not safe to travel in the mountains at night. There is a little shrine there," he thought to himself. Out loud he said, "Please allow me to stay here tonight."

He went into the shrine and laid himself down. But while he was sleeping, he heard a knock on the door. Then he heard a voice: "God of Mountain, god of Mountain, a baby is being born in the village. Let's go and decide her years."

Then from within the shrine, another voiced said, "Hello, god of Broom. Today I have a visitor and can't go out. I'm sorry, but can you go and do it alone?"

God of Broom outside said, "Very well, I will go alone."

Then all was silent.

昔

After a long while, almost dawn, the man heard a knock on the door again. "God of Mountain, I just came back. It was a baby girl. I gave her eighteen years to live. Was it suitable?"

From within the shrine, another voice answered, "Yes, that's good. That's good. Eighteen years is good. Thank you." Then it became quiet again.

The man thought, "Was it a dream, or real? It was very strange."

He got up. It was already light outside. He said to the shrine, "Thank you very much for letting me stay." And he went back home.

There, he found out that his wife had had a baby the night before. It was a baby girl. "Oh, no! So it was my daughter they were talking about last night. She will die at the age of eighteen!"

He became so sad. He told his wife. "Such and such happened. I was sleeping in a shrine last night, and heard this and that. She will die at eighteen."

His wife became sad, too. "It is a pity she will only live for eighteen years. I want a longer life for her." She cried and cried.

A traveling monk passing by heard her crying. "What's the matter?" He came in.

"Such and such happened. Our baby was born just last night. But we learned she would die at the age of eighteen. This is sad. This is so sad."

But the monk said, "I see. Here's what to do. Cook good food and pack it in a three-tier lunch box. Fill a bottle with sake, too. Then, carry them toward the west. Go on and on and on, straight west. You will see two old men playing *Go* (Japanese checkers) or *Shogi* (Japanese chess), but they are really gods. While they are playing, put the food into their mouths. Make them drink sake, too."

So the wife cooked tasty food, packed it, and wrapped the box with a carrying cloth. She filled a bottle to the top with sake. She started walking to the west. On and on and on she walked. And finally, she came to two Jisama playing Shogi. They had long beards.

"Oh, these old men must be the gods."

She sneaked up to them. Without a word, she unwrapped the cloth, opened the box, and poured sake into a cup. While they were playing Shogi, she put the cup in one Jisama's hand. Without looking, this Jisama drank it up. She picked up food with chopsticks and put it into his mouth. Then she put a sake cup in the other Jisama's hand. He, too, drank sake and ate food involuntarily. They were paying such strong attention to their game.

She poured more sake. She put more food into their mouths. It took a while, but finally, the Jisama noticed her.

"Oh, I was wondering how that good food was coming into my mouth. It was you. Thank you very much."

The wife said to the Jisama. "Such and such happened. My daughter's life is only eighteen years. It was declared. But somehow, could you make her live a little longer?"

The god said, "Oh, I see. You know, I shouldn't change it. But you gave us such wonderful food and sake. Let me see."

He took out something that looked like an old-fashioned account book and turned pages.

"Oh, here it is! The god of Broom decided on eighteen years. I'm sorry but I can't do anything about it."

"But please! How about more sake?" She poured more sake and fed him more food.

The god said, "Well, then. Pass me that brush and inkstone."

He borrowed a brush and inkstone from the other god. He added two strokes before the numeral for eighteen. Now, it read eighty-eight.

八十八

The wife thanked the god, "Thank you very much. Thank you very much."

She went home.

Her daughter lived a long life, up to eighty-eight.

Oshimai

昔

NOTE FROM FRAN: In the old number system, eighteen was written ten-eight, eighty was written eight-ten. So by writing another eight in front of eighteen, it became eighty-eight (eight-ten-eight).

テハ   ハテ   ハテハ
Eighteen   Eighty   Eighty-eight

God of Broom was associated with childbirth, helping to "sweep" the baby out.

COMMENT FROM MRS. FUJITA: There are similar stories about deciding people's years. A man learned he would die at fifteen. He was very careful. But a horsefly flew to him. And while he was paying attention to the horsefly, he cut himself with a chisel and died. Or while he was on a high place, a horsefly flew around him. He fell down, hit himself with an adz and died. These stories show that they could not avoid their fate.

Maybe Japanese gods are bribed easily. Or maybe Japanese people are not afraid of gods. There are many stories in which people outsmart the gods.

No Gods Here

INSIGHT: "Hair" is also *kami* in Japanese.

Once upon a time, a priest told his apprentice, "I'm going to visit my parishioner and read a sutra. Come with me right away."

Just then, the apprentice was going for a pee. But if he did not obey his master immediately, the master would scold him. So he followed his master right away. They left in such a hurry that they did not even bring hoods or hats to protect their shaven heads from the sun.

As the apprentice walked, his belly started to feel heavier and heavier. So he decided to pee at the roadside.

The master said, "Don't pee there. Every road belongs to *Doso-jin* (a roadside god). You must not pee at a place where a god is."

The apprentice was scolded and couldn't pee there. With a full belly, he followed the master.

They passed a farm.

"It should be OK to pee here," he thought. He began tucking up his kimono.

Then the master said, "Every farm belongs to *Hata-gami* (a farm god). He does mind it. Don't pee here."

The apprentice had to follow the master with full belly.

"Yes, yes! Soon we'll come to a river. I can pee there," he thought.

When the apprentice tucked up his kimono at the river, the master said, "Don't pee here. Every river belongs to *Mizu-gami* (a water god). Don't do that."

They rode a boat. They were going to the parishioner's home across the river.

On the boat, the apprentice couldn't wait any longer. His belly was so full.

"Where can I pee? Maybe in the corner of this boat." So he went to one corner of the boat and tucked up his kimono.

"Hey, you! Don't pee there. In every boat, there is *Fune-gami* (a boat god). Don't do that."

"Oh, I'm in a trouble. God on the roadside, god in the

farm, god in the water, and god on the boat. God here, god there, god everywhere. Is there any place where there is no god? No god. No kami. No kami. No hair!"

He found one place. He stood behind his seated master and peed on the master's shaved head.

Oshimai

昔

COMMENT FROM MRS. FUJITA: This priest is a Buddhist priest, but he also believed in the gods of Japanese Shintoism. I think this is one characteristic of Japanese people.

Not here, not there. The priest taught the apprentice "What not to do," but he did not teach him "What to do." It brought him this mess. Whenever I tell this story, I think back on myself, how I scolded my own children. I said many "No's" to them. Don't go. Don't do. I didn't tell them the alternative choice they could take. I was like the priest in this story. So I don't have any right to laugh at him. Even so, when I imagine what the priest would say after this, I cannot help but laugh.

JIZO STORIES

Little stone statues of Jizo, guardian of lost souls and protector of children and travelers, are common in Japan especially along roadsides. Jizo was the most common Buddhist image and, for that reason, it had a strong connection to people's lives.

Talking Jizo

Once upon a time, there was a Jizo-sama statue at the top of a mountain.

A young merchant was coming up from this way. And a little older merchant was coming up from the other way. Both of them sweating, the men met at the mountain top. They sat at the Jizo-sama and took a rest.

The older merchant had a successful business. He carried a lot of money tucked in his jacket. The young merchant saw it and said, "Oh Jisama, you are traveling on business, too? Did it go well?"

Jisama said, "Yes, this time it went very well."

They had a good talk and a good rest. Then they were about to start again, going in opposite directions. "So long."

But the young merchant suddenly felt like taking the old man's money. He stabbed Jisama with his short sword and killed him. He put Jisama's money in his jacket.

He felt like Jizo-sama was staring at him.

He said to the statue, "Don't tell anyone."

Then Jizo-sama replied, "I won't tell. But you will."

"Impossible! A stone Jizo-sama can't speak. I just killed a man. I must be hearing things."

The young man went his way, leaving the dead Jisama's body lying there. 昔

Ten or twenty years passed. That young merchant became old. He was going over that same mountain again. At the Jizo-sama, he saw a young merchant talking with the Jizo-sama.

"What are you doing?" asked the old man.

The younger man answered, "I felt like Jizo-sama was trying to tell me something, so I was listening hard."

"You are only imagining it. Once, I felt like this Jizo-sama was talking to me. But it's impossible."

"Really? You heard Jizo-sama once? When was it?"

"Well ... It was a long time ago. To tell you the truth, I once killed a merchant here. I felt like Jizo-sama was staring at me, so I said, 'Don't tell anyone.' And I thought I heard Jizo-sama say 'I won't tell, but you will.' But I don't think I really heard that. It's impossible."

Then the younger man said, "So it was you who killed my father! I come here often and talk with Jizo-sama. Jizo-sama kept telling me that someday the man who killed my father would come here and confess. So I have been waiting for a long, long time."

The younger man caught him and brought him to the magistrate's office.

Oshimai

Red Face Jizo

Once upon a time, there was a beggar man. Whenever he saw a statue of Jizo-sama, he went there carrying a pail of water and washed its face nice and clean with a bamboo brush. So he was called "face washing beggar" or "Jizo washing beggar."

He was not originally from Fukushima. When he was young, he lived in Sanriku, north of Fukushima.

By the seashore in Sanriku, there stood a Jizo-sama. The old village people used to say, "It has long been said that when this Jizo-sama's face turns red, our village will be destroyed."

Jizo-sama was made of stone, so it seemed impossible that its face could turn red.

One day, the young people were talking, "This Jizo-sama's face will never turn red. It's made of stone. But we can tease the others."

So they went to a mountain, brought back red clay, and daubed it on Jizo-sama's face.

The next day, the old people found Jizo-sama's face red but said, "Who has done this mischief?"

They brought pails of water and scrubbed the clay off the face. Jizo-sama's face was not red any more. "Good! Good!" They happily went back home.

昔

But one of the young ones was very mischievous. He said, "We took a lot of trouble making Jizo-sama's face red, but the old folks washed it away so easily. Red clay wasn't a good idea. I will make Jizo-sama's face red again, but this time, with something stronger."

He collected seeds of a dye plant, ground them, and painted Jizo-sama's face red with it.

The next day, the old people were surprised to see Jizo-sama's face very red. "Oh, no! But it might be some young man's doing again."

They all carried pails of water and started scrubbing the Jizo-sama's face. They scrubbed and scrubbed, but the dye was strong. Jizo-sama's face remained red.

The old people were shocked. "Jizo-sama's face turned red. It means this village is in danger. We have to go back home, pack our things, and evacuate to the hills nearby."

They packed their things, and started walking in a line out of the village.

That mischievous young man called to them from the top of the mountain, "It was I who made Jizo-sama's face red. I painted it with dye. You are great fools to be scared away."

The villagers said, "Oh, it was his doing then. Young men are so troublesome."

Saying so, they all went back to their home again.

Suddenly, a big *tsunami* (tidal wave) struck the village. The whole village was drawn into the water and drowned. The only survivor was that mischievous young man who was on the mountain top.

"The whole village was destroyed by the wave. My relatives are all gone. Everyone in the village is gone, because of me! I destroyed the whole village."

昔

He walked on and on, and finally he came to Fukushima.

He became a beggar. And whenever he saw a Jizo-sama, he couldn't help but wash its face nice and clean.

   Oshimai

昔

COMMENT FROM MRS. FUJITA: I heard that this story is about the famous Sanriku Tsunami in 1896.

Monkeys' Jizo

Once upon a time, there were Jisama and Basama. Jisama gathered firewood in a mountain. Every day, Basama made three rice balls for Jisama to take to the mountain.

The rice balls in those days were not like the ones we have today. We now make triangular rice balls. But in the old days, rice balls were called *yaki-meshi*. Heap up two bowls with rice, put them together and make a big rice ball. Squeeze the rice ball tight, grill it, spread miso and grill it again. Wrap it with a leaf such as *butterbur* or bamboo. It makes a tasty lunch.

Every day, Jisama took such yaki-meshi to a mountain. When the sun reached the middle of the sky, he would say, "Oh, it's noon. It's lunch time." And he would eat lunch.

But on that particular day, he felt tired. "I'll lie down for a minute before I eat."

He lay down with his head on his arms. While he was drowsing, a lot of monkeys came down the mountain.

"Look. There are rice balls. Let's eat them together."

The monkeys ate the rice balls Basama made for Jisama.

Jisama was watching it with his half-closed eyes, but thought, "This doesn't happen so often. Let them eat my rice balls."

He watched the monkeys eating his rice balls, with his eyes half closed, without saying anything. When monkeys finished the rice balls, young ones came toward Jisama. They climbed on his legs. They climbed on his arms. It tickled.

But Jisama thought, "This doesn't happen so often. Let them play."

Without saying anything, Jisama kept still. Soon, monkeys started climbing on his chest and belly. Some even jumped up and down, up and down on this belly. Jisama couldn't help breaking wind.

Bu!

The young monkeys were surprised at the sound.

"This said 'Bu!'"

They ran to where their father and mother and other adult monkeys were.

"That thing over there said 'Bu!' What's that?" they asked.

A wise old monkey said, "Bu means Buddha. That must be Buddha."

They all ran to it. Something like Buddha was lying down.

"Oh, Buddha! People abandoning your statue here like this is such a sin. We will bring you to the shrine in the mountain."

They raised the lying Buddha, made him clasp his hands and cross his legs. Then, they all started carrying him. On the way, there was a river. Crossing the river, they sang,

> "It's fine to wet the monkey's stones.
> "But let's not wet the Jizo's stones.
> "It's fine to wet the monkey's stones.
> "But let's not wet the Jizo's stones."

Singing, they carried Jisama.

"It's fine to wet the monkey's stones.
"But let's not wet the Jizo's stones."

The song was so funny, Jisama almost giggled. But he thought, "This doesn't happen so often. They think I'm Jizo. I don't want to disappoint them. I should keep quiet." He had to try very hard not to laugh.

Monkeys carried him to the shrine and set him in an alcove. They put their hands together and prayed. Some brought him nuts. Some brought him grapes. Some even brought him coins.

When they left, Jisama put the nuts, grapes, and coins in his jacket, crossed the river and went home. He told Basama, "Such and such happened, and the monkeys gave me all these. I couldn't eat my rice balls, but I got so much more."

Jisama and Basama were eating the nuts when Basama next door came in. "May I borrow fire?"

She slid the door open and saw Jisama and Basama eating good food. "Why? Where did you get those?" she asked.

"Such and such happened and the monkeys in the mountain ..." Jisama explained.

Basama next door said, "I must send my Jisama to the mountain then."

She hurried home. Jisama was just lying around in the house, doing nothing. She told him to get up. "You have to go to the mountain. I will make rice balls to take with you."

She cooked rice as quickly as she could, made rice balls, handed them to Jisama, and sent him out to the mountain. Jisama waited until the sun was in the middle of the sky. He wanted to eat the rice balls himself. But as his wife told him, he left them there and lay down. He waited.

Monkeys came down the mountain.

"Look, there are rice balls again. Let's eat them together."

Monkeys ate them. Then, one of them said, "Look! I was wondering where he went, but the Jizo we carried yesterday is back here. He is lying here again."

"It's a sin to leave him here like that. Let's bring him back to the shrine again."

They raised him up and carried him. As they crossed the river, they sang,

> "It's fine to wet the monkey's stones.
> "But let's not wet the Jizo's stones.
> "It's fine to wet the monkey's stones.
> "But let's not wet the Jizo's stones."

Jisama heard the song. It was so funny. He burst out, "Ha, ha, ha, ha!"

Monkeys were surprised. "He's not Jizo. He's a human!"

They threw him into the river and ran away. This Jisama got all wet and went home.

Basama was expecting nuts and coins. But what she got was the soaked Jisama.

Oshimai

KANNON

Kannon (*Quan Yin*) is associated with compassion. She was very popular among people just like Jizo-sama. She grants people their wish, and holds out her hand for them.

A Dream Millionaire

Once upon a time, there was a very religious farmhand, working for a millionaire. Every morning, he was turned out of bed and sent to the field so early that the stars were still in the sky. He had to work in the field until after sunset. Then he went back to his master's mansion and had to chop wood and heat the bath.

There were always more chores to do. When he finished them all and finally went to sleep, he was worn out like a rag. But he made it a rule to put his hands together and pray to Kannon-sama, the Goddess of Mercy, before he crept into his thin hard futon.

"Kannon-sama, Kannon-sama, I thank you. I was in fine health and could work well all day."

昔

When he was young, he could work very hard. But now, as he was getting older and his body weaker, he couldn't work as much as he used to. Now he was often scolded by his master.

"Oh, I hate being a farmhand. I wish I could be a millionaire, even just for one day. I want to sleep in a silk futon, wake up and wear a silk kimono and silk jacket. My breakfast tray would be filled with wonderful foods from mountain and sea. I would eat them and do nothing all day. Once in a while, when I would go out and check my fields, I would ask my men, 'Hi, how's your work?' What a nice life! I wish I could be a millionaire, even just for one day. Or if that's too much to ask, I wish I could be a millionaire in my dreams."

One night, after he prayed to Kannon-sama and crept into his futon, Kannon-sama appeared to him in his dream.

She said, "You are a religious man. I will make your wish come true. But I can't make you a real millionaire in the daytime. Instead, I can arrange for you to trade places with the millionaire in your dreams." Saying so, she disappeared.

Still dreaming, he put his hands together. "Thank you very much, Kannon-sama."

昔

The next day, as usual, he was turned out of his futon early in the morning and worked very hard all day. Finally it was time for bed. He put his hands together and prayed to Kannon-sama. Then he crawled into his thin hard futon and fell asleep right away.

That night, in his dream, he was a millionaire. He wore a silk kimono and silk jacket and sat on a big silk cushion. On the tray in front of him, he had rice heaped up like a mountain, soup and other dishes. A woman sat beside him and served sake.

"Wow, this is the life of a millionaire. It's so great. I'm so thankful," thought the man.

112

Then it was morning. He was thrown out of his futon and sent to the field. But he thought, "I might be able to be a millionaire again in my dream tonight."

As always, he had to work very, very hard, but the thought seemed to lighten his labor. That night, he put his hands together and prayed to Kannon-sama. Then he slept. In his dream, he was a millionaire again. The beautiful woman served sake. Also she massaged his shoulders. People around him took good care of him. So he just sat on the cushion, ate and lay down, then ate again and had a back massage.

"Oh, this is wonderful."

But morning came again. He was thrown out of his futon and sent to the field. That night, in his dream, he was a millionaire again. A luxurious hot tub of fragrant Japanese cypress was filled with steaming water. His usual bath was full of dirt, but this bath was overflowing with clean water. He soaked himself, and then climbed out. A beautiful woman came in and scrubbed his back. He went back to the tub and soaked himself again in the hot water until he felt dizzy. Then he came out again and got a massage on the back and shoulders. He was taken to a nice, soft futon.

"Will I dream in my dream?" he wondered, but then it was morning.

He was thrown out of his futon again and sent to the field. He had to work very hard during the daytime, but thinking he would be a millionaire in his dream, the work didn't seem so bad. He felt younger and stronger.

At first, he could only carry two bundles of wood, but now he could carry three. A nice bath, a good massage and good food in his dream seemed to make him stronger. He could work harder. His complexion was much better now.

昔

But on the contrary, his master the millionaire became paler and paler. During the daytime, he sat on a nice soft cushion, ate good food, and did nothing much except for going out to check his fields once in a while. But at night, while he slept in his soft silk futon, he was a farmhand in his dreams. He was thrown out of his thin hard futon early in the morning and sent to the field. He had to hoe the ground, but he wasn't used to it, so he hurt his foot with the hoe. He had to cut grass with a sickle, but he cut his hand with it. He had to make a bundle, but when he tied the rope, the soft skin on his hands peeled off. He was bending all day, so his back ached, too. He felt aches throughout his body.

"This is so hard. I'm so miserable. It hurts everywhere."

He suffered all night long. But it was all in his dream. So when he woke up in the morning, he had not a single scratch.

During the daytime, he sat on a silk cushion and ate good food. But still, he worried about night. He stayed up late, and tried not to sleep until he couldn't keep his eyes open any more. Then, he fell into the futon and again in his dream, he was a farmhand. With a hoe, he cut his feet. With a sickle, he cut his hands. When he weeded in the rice paddy, the pointed leaves pricked his eyes.

"It hurts here. It hurts there. I'm so miserable. I'm so sad."

He could only eat very poor food like millet, and watery soup with no ingredients, just thickened by flour. They tasted so bad that he couldn't eat any.

"I'm so hungry. It hurts everywhere. I'm so miserable."

He suffered all night long. When he woke up in the morning, there was much good food in front of him. But he was so scared of the night that even with the wonderful food in front of him, he couldn't eat.

He became thinner and thinner, paler and paler. He suffered and suffered, and finally passed away.

114

On the other hand, the farmhand only ate millet and thin soup in real life, but his complexion became better and better, and he became healthier and healthier. He lived long after the millionaire died. After many years, he went the way of nature, and died in peace.

Oshimai

昔

COMMENT FROM MRS. FUJITA: This story teaches us how important good sleep is for our health.

I am picky about food, but I can sleep anywhere. I can sleep in a flat, hard futon, or on a bench, or in a car. I can even sleep standing in a train. I can sleep in the light, or in the dark. I can sleep with or without noise. I think I am gifted with this skill, and it may be giving me my power.

Lizard and Scarab

Once upon a time, there was a lazy artist. He painted when he felt like it, but when he was not in the mood, he didn't paint at all. His painting style was difficult, too. So people didn't make many orders for his work. He became poorer and poorer, and was even running short of food.

But his friends knew that he could paint beautiful pictures. So they said, "How can we make him start working harder?"

"Maybe he will work hard when he gets a wife."

They found him a beautiful wife from the next village. But still, he didn't work much. His color box just sat there unopened.

115

His wife didn't know what to do. "I will ask Kannon-sama to make him start painting."

She visited a shrine every day for twenty-one days, praying, "Please, make my husband do his work. Make him open his color box and start painting."

She kept up her prayers for twenty-one days. On the twenty-first day when she returned home, she saw her husband taking a nap, as always.

But suddenly he woke and said, "Look! Look! A beautiful lizard is here."

"Where?" The wife looked around, but there was no lizard.

"There! Over there! Wow! It's a beautiful lizard. I wish I could make such a beautiful color." But saying so, he just went back to sleep.

"Oh, well. He is hopeless," sighed the wife.

But that night, the painter called his wife again and said, "Look! Look! A beautiful scarab beetle is here. Look at the color of its wings. I wish I could make a color like that."

"I don't see a scarab," said the wife.

But the painter insisted, "It's there! See? It's there!"

昔

The next day, in the daytime, the painter was saying, "A lizard! What a beautiful lizard!"

And that night, he was saying, "A scarab! What a beautiful scarab!"

The wife could see nothing. But it seemed that the painter could see a beautiful lizard during the daytime and a beautiful scarab at night. And wanting to make such beautiful colors, he opened his color box and started painting lizards and scarabs.

It was not easy to make such beautiful colors. He tried this and he tried that, and finally, he could make a very beautiful color.

116

One day, he got an order from a big temple: "Paint on a folding screen for us."

Every day, the painter painted on a screen using that beautiful color.

The priest was very pleased with his work and paid him a lot of money.

After that, people admired him as a great painter who could make a rare and beautiful color, and started ordering his paintings.

He became very rich.

But in the daytime, he kept seeing a lizard crawling in front of him. And at night, a scarab kept flying about. They were so beautiful.

"I can't concentrate when the lizard keeps crawling and the scarab keeps flying about. I can't paint quietly."

He smashed the lizard with a stick and killed it. At night, he smashed the busy scarab, too.

But after that, he could never make that beautiful color again.

Oshimai

TRAVELING PRIESTS

People used to believe that they should not treat a visitor unkindly, especially during the turn of the year. This belief comes from the Buddhist teaching that charity leads you to happiness, that the more charity you perform, the closer you are to heaven.

I don't know if they still do it, but when I was a child, the Buddhist temples had Sunday schools. A priest used to tell preaching stories to neighborhood children. The stories were almost always like the ones below, teaching us to be kind to a beggar-looking priest.

A Visitor on New Year's Eve

Once upon a time, there were Jisama and Basama. They were very, very poor. It was New Year's Eve. Jisama and Basama were talking. "We are so poor that we can't even make mochi to offer to God. We can at least offer the pounding sounds."

Jisama and Basama played a children's hand-clapping game about making mochi. They clapped their hands and made mochi-pounding sounds.

118

A wandering priest came by. "It sounds very happy here. Can I have one mochi?" he asked.

"Oh, we are sorry. It's just sounds we are making. We have no rice to pound into mochi. In fact, we have no food. But at least we have a nice warm hearth. Please come in and warm yourself."

So, the priest came in. They added more firewood for the priest. The priest said, "Thank you very much. Now I feel nice and warm."

Then Jisama said, "But Priest, look outside. It looks like snow. I think you had better stay here tonight. Look at the sky. It is getting dark. We are sorry we have no food. But we have fire, so you can sleep by the hearth."

"Thank you. I appreciate your kindness."

The priest lay down by the hearth. Jisama and Basama looked for some covering for the priest. They took off their jackets and covered the priest with them. Then they laid a straw mat on top. The priest slept like that.

昔

The next morning, it was New Year's Day. Basama woke up early. In the kitchen, she said, "I can't make any breakfast. But at least I can heat up some water. Jisama, Jisama, please go to the well and bring the first water of the year. We will drink hot water and welcome the New Year."

The first water on New Year's Day is special. Basama made a fire and heated it up. They stirred up the hearth and made the room really warm. Then, they began to wake the priest up.

"Priest, Priest, please wake up. It's New Year's Day."

But the priest didn't move.

"Priest, Priest, it's morning. It's New Year's Day. Please wake up."

Still, he didn't move an inch.

"Why? What's the matter?"

They uncovered the straw mat, and then their jackets.

There, they found a big lump of gold.

Oshimai

A Blind Visitor on New Year's Eve

Once upon a time, there lived a very rich man and his wife. And not far from there, lived poor Jisama and Basama.

One New Year's Eve, a priest came to the rich couple's house. He was *Zatobo-sama*, a blind priest. With the help of a cane, he walked to the door and asked, "Will you let me stay here tonight?"

But the rich man said, "Tomorrow is New Year's Day. We have just finished our cleaning. We don't want a filthy person like you here tonight. Now, get out!"

Zatobo-sama went on and came to the door of poor Jisama and Basama. He asked them, "Will you let me stay here tonight?"

Jisama and Basama said, "We don't have any food to offer you. But if you don't mind, please stay."

They invited him in and let him sleep by the warm hearth. The next morning, Zatobo-sama woke up and said, "Thank you very much for letting me stay here. As a token of my thanks, I want to draw the first water for you."

But Jisama and Basama said, "No! You are blind. You might fall into the well. Please don't do it."

"I'll be very careful. Let me draw the first water."

Zatobo-sama insisted. So Jisama and Basama handed him a bucket. Zatobo-sama went toward the well, finding his way with his cane.

"Will he be able to bring the first water all right?"

They were worried and waited. Then they heard a splash. "Oh, no! Zatobo-sama must have fallen down the well!"

Jisama and Basama hurried toward the well. Just as they feared, Zatobo-sama was deep down in the well. He was holding on to the well bucket.

"Hold on, Zatobo-sama. We will pull you up."

Jisama and Basama pulled the bucket rope, singing, "Yo-ho! Yo-ho!"

Zatobo-sama in the well sang too, keeping the rhythm.

"Yo-ho! Yo-ho! Draw up good fortune! Yo-ho! Yo-ho! Draw up good fortune!"

Jisama and Basama pulled, saying, "Yo-ho! Yo-ho! Draw up good fortune!"

But when they had pulled it up, they found no Zato-bo-sama in the bucket. Instead, there sat a big cake of mochi.

Jisama and Basama happily presented it on the family altar to celebrate the New Year. Then they cut the mochi to eat, and inside the mochi, they found gold coins!

昔

The rich man and his wife heard the story. They envied Jisama and Basama.

"Next time a priest comes, I will bring him home and make him stay no matter what," they decided.

They waited for a couple of days. There came another Zatobo-sama. This Zatobo-sama was in a hurry. He was walking fast.

"Zatobo-sama, Zatobo-sama, please stay at our house tonight," said the rich man.

"No, I'm rather in a hurry. I have to get to the next village, so I can't stay here."

"No, no, you are going to stay here." He forced Zatobo-sama into his house, made him stay overnight, and fed him well.

The next morning, he said, "Zatobo-sama, I know it's too late for the first water, but go to the well and bring us water."

"No, I'm blind. I don't want to go to the well and bring water," said Zatobo-sama.

"No, no, you're going," he insisted.

"I might fall into the well. I don't want to go," said Zatobo-sama.

"Just go!"

Zatobo-sama had no choice. He went to the well. He was carefully lowering the bucket when the rich man pushed him down into the well.

"Help! Help!" yelled Zatobo-sama.

"Zatobo-sama, you have to say 'Yo-ho! Yo-ho!'" said the rich man.

"Yo-ho! Yo-ho!" Zatobo-sama said.

"Yo-ho! Yo-ho!" prompted the rich man.

"Yo-ho! Thick! Yo-ho! Gooey! Yo-ho! Thick! Yo-ho! Gooey!" came from the well.

The rich man thought, "Oh, he must be talking about mochi. Thick, gooey mochi is coming up." He pulled it up.

In the well bucket was a heap of cow dung.

Oshimai

Daishi and Forked Daikons

INSIGHT: *Kobo Daishi* (774-835) was a
famous priest in Japan. He was said to travel
throughout Japan teaching Buddhism to
the people. There are many stories of him
throughout Japan. *Kobo-samma* is celebrated
on *Daishi-ko* day, which is November 27 in
Fukushima Prefecture, other winter dates in
other areas.

Once upon a time, a girl was washing *daikons* by a river. A
filthy looking priest came by. He looked like a beggar. He
said to the girl, "I'm very hungry. Would you give me one of your
daikons?"

The girl said, "I would very much like to give you one.
But my master is a miser. He counted all these daikons before he
handed them to me. If I give you one, he will know it instantly and
he will scold me a lot. I can't give you one. But ..."

She found a forked daikon. "This one daikon looks like
two. I think I can give you half of it." She broke off one branch and
gave it to the priest.

This priest was Kobo-sama.

He said, "You will have a lot of forked daikon in this area
so that a poor person like you can share it with a poor person like
me."

昔

So, after that, they had a lot of forked daikons in that area.

On Daishi-ko Day, they made it a rule to offer forked daikons.

Oshimai

Covering Snow

Once upon a time, a priest came to the door of a very poor Basama. He asked, "May I stay here tonight?"

Basama said, "Of course! Please come in."

She brought him in and said, "I have nothing to offer you, but at least there is a fire in the hearth. Please warm yourself."

She added firewood, and the priest enjoyed the warm fire. Then his stomach growled. Basama could hear it. She wanted to offer him some food, but she had nothing.

She went out to a vegetable field next to her house. It was not her field, it belonged to her rich neighbor. But she stole a daikon from there. She cooked it and offered it to the priest.

The priest said, "This daikon is very good. Basama, let's eat it together."

But Basama said, "No. You can eat it, because you are a priest. But I can't. This daikon is stolen from my neighbor's vegetable field. He will send his servant to me tomorrow. If I tell him that I only served it to a priest, he wouldn't arrest me. But if I eat it with you, I will be a real thief. I can't eat it with you. Please eat it all by yourself."

"Don't worry. This is a very good daikon. Let's share it

together."

The priest begged her many, many times. But Basama insisted, "No, if I eat it, I will be arrested as a thief tomorrow. I shouldn't eat it."

The priest said, "No, don't worry. It is going to snow a lot tonight. It will cover all your footprints. You are not a thief. So, don't worry and let's share this daikon."

Finally, they ate the daikon together.

昔

Around midnight, it started snowing. *Non, non, non, non, non, non, non, non.* (sound of falling snow)

Don, don, don, don, don, don, don, don (snowing harder), it covered the footprints in the daikon field. So in the morning, nobody noticed that Basama had stolen a daikon.

This priest was, in fact, Kobo-sama.

Even today, it snows on Daishi-ko night.

And on that night, the poor might steal from someone else's vegetable field without getting caught.

Oshimai

Kobo Spring

Once upon a time, there was a village in Aizu that had no water. They had no water to irrigate rice fields. They had no water to drink. The village sat halfway up the mountain, so they had to go down to the mountain stream and carry up all the water they needed.

125

Naturally, water was very precious in the village. They only took a bath once or twice a year. And when they did, they only used a bucketful of water to wash and wipe off their body. Such a village it was.

One day, a priest in rags came to that village. Visiting each house, he asked, "I'm thirsty. May I have a cup of water?"

Everyone said, "We have no water to give you."

But finally, he was given a little water at a house. He sipped the water once and said, "This is not cold. Don't you have cold water?"

A girl in the house said, "Please wait."

She took the empty buckets and went down the mountain. I'm not sure how long it took, but after a while, she brought up cold water from the mountain stream and offered it to the priest.

The priest asked her, "You have no water in this village?"

The girl answered, "No, when we need water, we have to go all the way down the mountain to the stream."

"To thank you for that good water, I'll find a water source somewhere in this village."

He walked around, tapping the ground with his walking stick. He tapped here and there. Then, he came to a spot where a hole opened when he tapped the ground. And out from the hole, fresh cool water started to flow.

They named it Kobo Spring. Even today, the villagers are gratefully drinking the water from that spring.

Oshimai

Kobo and Stone Potato

Once upon a time, there was a Basama. She was washing potatoes by a river.

A priest in rags came by. "Those look like good potatoes. I'm very, very hungry. Would you be kind enough to give me one or two of them?"

The Basama didn't want to give him even one potato. She said, "Oh, these potatoes are so hard, like stones. They are not good enough to offer to a priest like you." She kept scrubbing the potatoes.

The priest asked her again, "Well, I don't mind if it is a bit hard. Would you give me one?"

But Basama said, "No, these are as hard as stones. I'm afraid it might break your teeth."

She scrubbed again and then, when she finished, she carried them home, threw them into a pot and started cooking.

She cooked and cooked but the potatoes wouldn't soften.

She cooked and cooked and cooked and cooked. But the potatoes were as hard as stones.

After that, in Basama's village, they never could grow good potatoes. All they could get were as hard as stones.

Oshimai

UNCANNY TALES

Gourd Cave

O nce upon a time, a traveler was walking along a river. He saw
a beautiful lady trying to scoop up water with a gourd. But
the water was quite far below and though the lady was trying, she
couldn't reach the water. She looked at a loss.

The traveler saw it, and put down his backpack. "Let me
help. I will get it for you."

He held onto a tree with one hand and with the other, he
took the gourd. He crouched down and tried to reach water. From
that low position, he could see a deep cave under the river bank.

As soon as he saw the cave he felt like going there. Drawn
by some force, he walked deep into the cave. And the lady was
following him, too.

He came to a little village where beautiful plum, peach, and
cherry blossoms were in full bloom all at the same time. It was the
lady's village.

At her house, he was entertained warmly. The food was
good.

Day after day, he had fun singing and dancing.

昔

Three years passed and one day, the man finally said, "I want to go home."

"I see," said the lady.

And she ushered him back, holding his hand and walking through the cave.

Then he found himself at the riverside, holding onto a tree with one hand, and a gourd with the other. His backpack was still there.

He had the gourd, but the lady was gone.

Oshimai

昔

COMMENT FROM MRS. FUJITA: This kind of mysterious village, in a deep cave as in this story, or behind a waterfall, or deep in the mountains in spring time, or under the sea, is a place where a village man or a traveler arrives by chance. It is a beautiful Shangri-La where the passage of time is different. It's a place where the man can't return even if he wants to. Most of the time it is a Shangri-La for men, with a beautiful lady.

Extracting Grease

Once upon a time, there was a foolish, lazy young man. He was saying, "I don't like working. Isn't there any job where I can eat and sleep and get paid?"

His father heard this and became angry. He said, "Eat and sleep and get paid? There is no such job. Ask anyone. There is no way you can make money doing that."

The foolish son went around, asking, "Isn't there any job where I can eat and sleep and get paid? Isn't there any job where I can eat and sleep and get paid?"

A man came toward him and said, "Yes, there is a job where you can get paid to eat and sleep."

"That's nice! I want that job. Where can I get that job?" asked the foolish son.

"I will take you there."

The man took the foolish son. They went over a mountain and came to a house. The man said, "Go in and wait. Soon, they will bring you wonderful food."

The foolish son sat and waited. A beautiful young lady came in and brought him a lot of botamochi. Then, she brought him a big dish of cooked potatoes, beans, and burdock. She brought him fish boiled with soy sauce. She brought him cooked bamboo shoots and bracken. The rice bowl was filled heaping full. The foolish son ate and ate and slept. Then, the beautiful lady came in again and said, "Please eat more. Please drink more."

The foolish son was very happy. He ate and ate and slept. He ate and ate and slept. But after three days, he got bored.

"Phew! I don't want to eat any more. Now, I want to go back home to see my parents."

But the lady said, "No, you wanted to eat and sleep. That's what you came here for. You have to eat. Eat more."

She brought botamochi again. He was full of botamochi already. But she insisted that he eat more. He ate so much that when he lay down, he felt sick and couldn't sleep. Feeling awful, he went outside. Right behind the house, he found another building.

He heard moaning coming from the building. "Ummm. Ummm."

"What is that?"

He looked in. There was a big fire. On that fire was a big pot. Over that big pot, a fat man was hung upside-down from the ceiling beam. His arms and legs were tied.

"Umm. It's hot. It's so hot. Ummm."

As he moaned, the fat man was sweating a greasy sweat. His grease was being collected in the pot below. It looked so painful.

Shocked, the foolish son ran away.

Oshimai

Yamanji and the Actor

INSIGHT: *Yamanji*, Mountain Jisama, is a creepy one-eyed character who can read your thoughts.

A traveling actor was walking through the mountains alone, rehearsing his lines for tomorrow in his head. He noticed a ragged, one-eyed Jisama walking behind him. "That's a strange Jisama that is following me," he thought.

From behind, that Jisama said, "You've just thought, 'That's a strange Jisama that is following me.' Haven't you?"

But the actor didn't care. He had to remember his lines for tomorrow.

"Here, my partner cries out, 'No!'"

From behind, Jisama said, "You've just thought, 'Here, my partner cries out, No!' Haven't you?"

"Then, I shake my fist."

Jisama said, "You've just thought, 'Then, I shake my fist.' Haven't you?"

The actor didn't care. "My partner goes, 'Don't be so ridiculous.' And she starts sobbing."

"You've just thought, 'My partner goes, 'Don't be so ridiculous.' And she starts sobbing.' Haven't you?"

"Then, she begs for mercy."

"You've just thought, 'Then, she begs for mercy.' Haven't you?"

"Here, I have my line. 'I can't forgive you. You made me lose face.' And I knock her down."

From behind, "You've just thought, 'I can't forgive you. You made me lose face.' And I knock her down' Haven't you?"

The actor thought, "Then, help comes. I'm about to drop my fist."

From behind, "You've just thought, 'Then, help comes. I'm about to drop my fist.' Haven't you?"

But the actor didn't care. He was concentrating so hard on his lines. "He says, 'Wait!'"

"He says, 'Wait!'"

"Then, I pick up a stick and hit my partner hard."

At this, The actor picked up a stick and hit the Jisama on the head.

"I have more to learn about these unpredictable mortals," Jisama said and ran away.

Oshimai

Mr. Red Cat

Once upon a time, there was an old man who had a very gentle cat. The cat's fur was red-gold with dark stripes, so he named it *Tora* (tiger).

Tora grew bigger and bigger but was still a gentle cat—at least, in front of its master.

One night, the man woke up and found his cat creeping off the futon which they shared every night. "What's the matter with him? Where is he going?" he wondered.

While he watched, Tora reached up with a claw and took down a *mame-shibori* towel (a cotton cloth printed with pea-sized dots), which the man always hung at the door.

Tora threw the towel over one shoulder and went out.

Jisama was worried about his red cat, so he followed, careful not to be seen. Tora didn't notice the man but went on and on.

Soon Jisama heard the sound of drum and flute, coming from the woods at Hachiman Shrine.

"What is happening? Today is not a festival of any kind."

He listened carefully to the song:

> KIK kata DON, KIK kata DON. (sound of
> drumming)
> Without Mr. Red Cat,
> We can't dance.
> KIK kata DON, KIK kata DON.

They sang like that.

> Without Mr. Red Cat,
> We can't dance. Ha!
> KIK kata DON, KIK kata DON.

Then the man's red cat Tora arrived, with the spotted towel tied around his head as a sweatband. All the cats rejoiced.

Tora explained, "My Jisama didn't fall asleep easily tonight. I couldn't get out of the house."

Then Tora walked up to the drum and started drumming. All the other cats started to dance and sing.

> KIK kata DON, KIK kata DON.
> Attack *Oharu*? Or attack *Omatsu*?
> KIK kata DON, KIK kata DON.
> Attack Oharu? Or attack Omatsu?
> KIK kata DON, KIK kata DON.

They sang and danced.

Jisama wondered, "What do they mean? Attack Oharu, or attack Omatsu? We have girls named Oharu and Omatsu in our village. But what does this song mean?"

Wondering, he left. He went back to his futon and waited patiently for his cat.

Before dawn, Tora came back quietly. It hung the towel, which was wet with sweat and dew, back in place. As if nothing had happened, it slipped into the futon, right beside the old man.

昔

When morning came, Tora meowed and rubbed against the man, as gentle and cute as ever.

But that night also, it again slipped out of the futon, threw the mame-shibori towel over one shoulder, and went off to the Hachiman Shrine. The man followed the cat. Again, he heard the song.

> KIK kata DON, KIK kata DON.
> Attack Omatsu?
> KIK kata DON, KIK kata DON.

Then they called different names, like,

> Attack *Oito*?

and

> Attack *Otake*?

They called different names and sang,

> KIK kata DON, KIK kata DON.

The old man got worried.

So the next morning, he went to talk to a temple priest. "Priest, Priest, every night my red cat, Tora, goes out and dances with other cats who are singing such a strange song. I wonder what all this means."

The priest listened and said, "I see, I see. As long as they call different names, like Oharu and Omatsu, it should be all right. But when they start calling one particular name, you must come to tell me."

昔

Jisama obeyed the priest. Every night he followed his red cat. Then one night, the cats started to sing,

> KIK kata DON, KIK kata DON.
> The daughter of *Kono-kono-bei*!
> KIK kata DON, KIK kata DON.
> The daughter of Kono-kono-bei!
> KIK kata DON, KIK kata DON.
> We've finally decided!
> KIK kata DON, KIK kata DON.

The man thought, "Well, tonight, they only called 'the daughter of Kono-kono-bei.' I have no idea who that is, but I had better go and tell this to the priest."

昔

The next morning, he went to the priest. In their village, there was no man called Kono-kono-bei. "Who is this Kono-ko-no-bei? Who is he? If we can't find him by tonight, his daughter might be attacked."

They thought and thought, but they couldn't figure it out. "Who is this Kono-kono-bei? Who can it be?"

The sun had set. It started to get dark. Then the priest hit upon an idea. "Oh, it must be *Mago-bei!* Ko-no-ko is a child of a child—a grandchild, *mago!* So they must have meant Mago-bei. They might attack Mago-bei's daughter."

They hurried to Mago-bei's house.

"It's just cats' talk, we're not sure if it means anything. But anyway, may we stay here tonight?" they asked Mago-bei.

They waited and waited as the night went on.

They didn't tell Mago-bei's daughter anything. So, as always, she was sleeping alone in her little room.

Midnight passed. It was about the Hour of the Ox—2 a.m., when evil things usually happen.

"*Nyao.*"

"*Nyago.*"

"*Nya-own!*"

They heard the meowing of cats. It got louder and more fierce.

"*Nyago, nyago, nyago, nyago!*"

It increased and increased. Then, they heard the bedroom door open with a big bang.

"Now!" The priest, Jisama, Mago-bei and every man in their

village dashed into the house.

There was a terrible battle.

They killed all the cats.

昔

In the morning, they dug a big hole and buried all the cats—except the old man's red cat, Tora. They couldn't find it anywhere.

"What happened to that cat?" they wondered.

昔

One year passed. Two years passed.

One day, a traveling monk came to their village. He visited a very poor man who lived at the outskirts of the village.

The monk asked, "Please, kindly give me a cup of tea."

He looked hungry, too, so the man wanted to offer him some food as well. But this poor man had no food at home. He went out behind his house. On a hillside, he found a pumpkin vine growing although nobody had planted it. It was growing strongly, and bore a huge pumpkin.

"Oh, good. Oh, good. I'm glad I found this. I'll cook this pumpkin and offer it to the monk." The poor man took the pumpkin home.

He showed it to the monk and said, "I'll cook this pumpkin for you."

With a knife, he cut the pumpkin in half. There were no seeds inside!

"No seeds? Where did you get this?" the monk asked.

"I went behind my house, looking for something to serve you. I found this wild pumpkin, and took it home."

"I see, I see. Let's take a look where it came from."

So, the monk and the man went behind the house and followed the pumpkin vine. It came from a spot on the bank.

"Dig at this place," the monk told the man.

The man dug at the spot. The roots went deep underground.

Finally, they found that it was coming from the eye socket of a cat's skull.

Bits of red fur still clung to it.

The monk said, "Seedless crops are not natural. You must not eat them. If you eat them, they might curse you. You must not eat seedless fruits or vegetables."

Oshimai

昔

COMMENT FROM MRS. FUJITA: I still hesitate a little when I eat seedless grapes and watermelons. They violate natural laws. I feel uneasy to eat them.

By the way, in the refrain *KIK kata DON, kikkata* is the sound made by hitting the metal rim of a drum with sticks. *Don* is the sound of hitting the drumhead.

I was taught never to say bad things about cats in front of them, because cats that grow bigger than the size of a human baby can understand human words and transform themselves into evil things. There were also many other warnings about cats, such as, "When cats walk near the dead, the dead start to dance," "Cats will curse you if you make them dance by covering their heads with bags," and "It's bad to show a mirror to cats."

We had so many negative sayings about cats because, although they were very close to us, they had a mysterious habit of gathering at night. Some say that cats go for training to *Neko-ma-ga-dake* (literally: cat-evil-high-mountain) where they learn human language and how to transform themselves into evil things. Then, they would revenge themselves upon humans for their oppression. In Fukushima, there is a mountain called Neko-dake, so I suppose cats go there for their training.

I imagine Red Cat in this story had finished his training at Neko-ma-ga-dake.

Ghost With Dignity

Once upon a time, there was a merchant. We don't know what his business was, but he made a big fortune. He wanted to live with dignity, so he built a gorgeous mansion. He moved into the mansion.

But in his newly built mansion, he felt uneasy. He was uncomfortable. Everywhere he looked, there was no dignity.

So he went to a wise man for advice.

"Even if you have a gorgeous house, it's not enough. You must have a status name, in order to have dignity in your house."

"Then, I need to get a new name," the man thought. He brought lots of gifts to a Samurai and in turn, was given a new name that sounded high class.

"Now my house has dignity."

昔

The merchant sat in his mansion satisfied and looked around. But still, he felt uneasy. He went to the wise man for more advice.

"In a house with dignity lives a man with dignity. And a man with dignity must have swords at his waist," was his advice.

So, the merchant brought more gifts to the Samurai, and was given permission to wear swords.

He came home with swords at his waist, sat in his mansion satisfied and looked around. But still, he couldn't see dignity in his house.

昔

He went to the wise man again.

"I've tried, but still there is no dignity in my new house. What do you think?"

"Well, a house with dignity cannot be achieved alone. Without a wonderful garden, it won't succeed," was his answer.

"I see, I see."

The merchant made a wonderful garden. He made a pond and arranged rocks. It was a beautiful garden. From the verandah and from indoors, he looked at his garden.

Still, he didn't see any dignity in his house.

"Oh, well, what can I do?"

昔

He went to the wise man again.

The wise man thought hard.

"Well ... a house with dignity can't be built in a day. It must stand there for many years, from generation to generation. It must be a house your father and grandfather lived and died in. They must remain there as ghosts, protecting you. The existence of those ghosts gives your house dignity. What your house lacks is these ghosts," he said.

"I see, I see. In a house with dignity, there must be ghosts."

昔

The merchant went to a temple and asked the priest, "I want ghosts to live in my house. How can I get ghosts?"

"Go to the graveyard behind this temple at night. You'll see many ghosts there. You can pick any ghosts you like," the priest answered.

That night, the merchant went to the graveyard and waited.

"Ghosts, ghosts, who wants to live in my house?" he asked loudly.

A ghost tottered toward him. "I want to live in your house," the ghost said.

"Very well, come with me."

Then the ghost of a woman tottered to him. "I want to live in your house, too," she said.

"Oh, you can come, too."

Then a strong looking ghost came.

"Please come to my house," the man asked the ghost.

He took three ghosts. They started to live in his house.

昔

But still, there was no dignity.

He returned to the temple and complained to the priest, "I brought three ghosts from your graveyard, but still my house lacks dignity."

The priest asked, "From which graves did they come?"

He studied the man's answer for a while. "A-ha! The one from this grave was a thief and was executed. This wasn't good. The woman from this grave was killed because she fled her husband with another man. And that man! He was a bandit!"

昔

So those ghosts turned out to be bad ones.

"Well, with these ghosts, my house can't earn dignity. I need a ghost with dignity to live in my house. A ghost with dignity. A ghost with dignity that suits my house. How can I get a ghost with dignity?"

He thought and thought.

"That's it!"

He threw a rope over a beam in his newly built house and hanged himself.

He became a ghost himself and lived in the house.

Since then, the house became a house with great dignity.

Oshimai

昔

COMMENT FROM MRS. FUJITA: In the Edo period (1603-1867), the government made a class system. Samurai were the highest class, farmers the second class, craftsmen the third, merchants the fourth. Though merchants made fortunes, they were looked down upon as the lowest class.

The dignity of a house is not just a matter of size. It is not just a matter of the amount of money people put into it. It is not just a matter of luxury or elegance. It should have the feeling of time, heritage, dignity, and deepness. A house with dignity cannot be built in a day. A newly rich man cannot build it, even if he is willing to pay for it. It needs a history.

From: Upper residence of Matsudaira Tadamasa
As depicted in the Edo-zu byōbu screens—17th century

STORIES OF ANIMALS

Two Rival Snakes

Once upon a time in a certain place, there were two mountains and on the first mountain there lived a baby snake. He was small, so he ate some bugs, and he grew bigger and bigger—enough to eat a frog and a mouse.

He grew bigger and bigger—enough to eat a rabbit and a weasel.

He grew bigger and bigger—enough to eat a fox and a monkey.

At last he grew bigger and bigger and bigger—enough to eat a deer and a wild boar.

And he curled his huge body around the first mountain and took a nap.

昔

On the second mountain there lived another baby snake. At first he was small, so he ate some bugs, and he grew bigger and bigger—enough to eat a frog and a mouse.

He grew bigger and bigger—enough to eat a rabbit and a weasel.

He grew bigger and bigger—enough to eat a fox and a monkey.

And at last he grew up bigger and bigger and bigger—enough to eat a deer and a wild boar.

But he had eaten everything on his mountain.

So that snake raised his head and looked for a nice place to get some more food. It looked as if the first mountain had a lot of deer and wild boars on it. "Good, I will move there."

So that second snake came down from his mountain,

> *zuru zuru, nyoro nyoro* (sound of a snake slithering),

to the first snake's mountain,

> zuru zuru, nyoro nyoro.

The first snake woke up, saw the other snake and said, "What did you come here for?"

The second snake said, "I'm going to live here. So get out, please."

"What are you talking about? I have lived here since I was born, so I can't leave. You! Go back where you came from!"

"No, I came here from far away. I can't go back. You get out."

"No, I won't move. You go back!"

"No, you get out!"

They were arguing so hard, the second snake bit the tail of the first snake, *am!* (biting sound)

But the first snake couldn't give up, so it bit the tail of the second snake, *am!*

The two big snakes made a big circle, head to tail, head to tail.

But they wouldn't stop fighting, and they wouldn't stop

144

biting am am am,

> and again and again, am am am,
> and am am am ...

They were big snakes. I don't know how long it took them, but after biting each other's tails many times, am am am and am am am ...

> only the two heads were left.

The second snake said, "I can't give up" and opened his mouth as large as he could with his last strength. But the first snake said, "I can't give up either," and opened his mouth as large as he could.

> And so—they ate each other up.
> There was nothing left at all.
> *Oshimai*

昔

COMMENT FROM MRS. FUJITA: "I am going to destroy you but I destroy myself in the end." There are many examples like that in this world, don't you think?

NOTE FROM FRAN: This simple fable looks like it's for children, but adults can appreciate it more deeply.

Messenger & Serpent

One day a lord who lived in the east country wanted to send a letter. He hired a messenger to deliver his letter to a lord who lived across the mountains in the west country.

In the old days, there were no post offices like we have now. When people wanted to send a letter to someone, they had to hire a messenger to deliver it. He would run along the country roads, carrying the letter in a box at the end of a long pole over his shoulder.

This messenger was very serious. He put the letter in the box, carried it on his shoulder, and ran,

> Sutakora sassa, sutakora sassa. (sound of
> running footsteps)

He didn't look to the right, he didn't look to the left, he didn't look up or down. He only looked in the direction he was running, and he ran,

> Sutakora sassa, sutakora sassa.

昔

On the way to the mountain pass there was a huge snake, which people called an *Uwabami.*

When Uwabami raised his head and looked around for food, he found it was coming up the hill ... He realized that the food would come into his mouth if he simply waited in the path with his mouth wide open. He waited.

As I told you before, the messenger didn't look to the right, he didn't look to the left, he didn't look up or down. He only looked in the direction he was running, and he ran,

Sutakora sassa, sutakora sassa.

So he ran straight into Uwabami's mouth without knowing what it was,

Sutakora sassa, sutakora sassa.

Uwabami swallowed him right down, *PaKU!* (Gulp)

The messenger thought, "I wonder why it is getting so dark? Why is the road so hard to run on? Maybe it's going to rain. Mud will make running even harder. I'd better hurry up."

So he ran and ran and ran in the long body of the Uwabami,

Sutakora sassa, sutakora sassa.

He ran right out the end,

Sutakora sassa, sutakora sassa.

昔

It was Uwabami's turn to be surprised, because the good food he caught had vanished. So he got ahead of the messenger and waited again with his mouth open in the middle of the road.

The messenger ran into Uwabami's mouth again without knowing where he was,

Sutakora sassa, sutakora sassa.

And Uwabami swallowed him down, PaKU!

The messenger thought that it was getting dark again and it looked like rain, so he hurried up,

Sutakora sassa, sutakora sassa.

He ran and ran and ran through the body of Uwabami,

and went out the other end again.

昔

The flustered Uwabami hurried ahead to ambush him again, and lay in wait with open mouth.

> Sutakora sassa, sutakora sassa. The
> messenger ran into the mouth again.
> PaKU!

And again, Sutakora sassa, sutakora sassa, the messenger ran out the other end.

And Uwabami said, "I had better gird up my loins!"

Oshimai

昔

COMMENT FROM MRS. FUJITA: In old times, both in Japan and in Europe, men's underwear was a loincloth: a long cloth wound around the waist and between the legs. It was wrapped tighter for hard or dangerous work.

The Japanese punchline literally means, "I must tighten my loincloth." Like "gird up your loins" in English (which also literally means "tighten your loincloth"), it has the additional meaning of "prepare to try harder." So the snake planned to try harder—which would block off the exit ...

The Frog Priest

INSIGHT: Japanese frogs say *gero gero* and
gokku-rakku. Since *Gokuraku* means "heaven,"
a frog is a suitable priest.

Once upon a time, there was a mysterious lotus pond. Every day the right number of lotus flowers bloomed for the day's funerals. If there were going to be two funerals, two flowers bloomed. If three flowers bloomed, there were going to be three funerals. Such a mysterious lotus pond it was.

In that pond lived the Frog Priest. Every morning, the first thing he did after he woke up was to climb up onto a lotus leaf, look around, and count the flowers.

"Today, there is one flower. We'll have one funeral today."

Or, "Oh, we are going to have three funerals today. There are three flowers."

And he would prepare for the funerals.

昔

One morning, he went up on a lotus leaf and looked around as always. He saw many flowers.

"What is this? There are so many flowers today. One, two, three, there is four, and there are more under the leaves, five, six ... oh, seven! There will be seven funerals today. Well, I should be prepared."

The Frog Priest put on his robe and stole. Before he

finished putting on his stole, here came Mrs. Mole running. "Frog Priest, Frog Priest, my husband passed away last night."

"What happened? I saw your husband working hard yesterday. He was working hard digging, wasn't he?"

"That's right. But while he was working hard, he dug through to the other side and met the shining sun. He got dazed. He came back home, but at night his head started to ache. 'That stupid sun, that stupid sun,' he cursed the sun. This morning, when I woke up, I found him dead. He was cursing the sun so badly last night, I'm afraid he won't be able to go to heaven."

"Oh, no, don't worry. Your husband Mr. Mole was such a hard worker. He would certainly not go down to hell. He will go to heaven. But just to make sure, I will chant a sutra for heaven. If you are worried, sit there and listen."

The Frog Priest started to chant.

> Gero, gero, gero, gero, *Nanmaidah.*
> Gero, gero, gero, gero,
> Gokku-RAKku, gokku-RAKku
> *Chiiin!!* (sound of a bell rung to signal the
> end of the prayer)

Mrs. Mole was happy.

"Thank you very much. I have to hurry and get home before the sun comes up." She hurried home.

昔

Soon, there came Mrs. Sparrow. "Frog Priest, Frog Priest, my baby child fell from our nest and died. He was such a baby, he won't know the way to heaven."

"Oh no, no. That child did nothing wrong in his short life. Jizo-sama will come to him, and carry him on his palm to heaven. But if you are still worried, I will chant a sutra for heaven. Sit there and listen."

He started his sutra again.

Gero, gero, gero, gero, Nanmaidah.
Gero, gero, gero, gero,
Gokku-RAKku, gokku-RAKku
Chiiin!!

Mrs. Sparrow went happily back home.

昔

Then there came Lady Carp. "Frog Priest, Frog Priest, my brother was caught today. He was greedy and put everything in his mouth. So he was caught by the fisherman. My brother was always hungry. Can he go up to heaven?"

"Oh, yes. It's very natural that young people are hungry all the time. By now, he must have been bravely killed on a cutting board. I will chant a sutra for heaven. Sit there and listen."

Gero, gero, gero, gero, Nanmaidah.
Gero, gero, gero, gero,
Gokku-RAKku, gokku-RAKku
Chiiin!!

Lady Carp swam back home.

昔

Leaning on a walking stick, there came Old Mrs. Gecko slowly. "Frog Priest, Frog Priest, my husband finally is out of his misery."

"Oh, yes. He lived in pain for so long. Finally he is released. I'm glad it's over."

"Well, there is still one thing. When he was young, he was a bad fellow. He drank a lot, gambled, and gave money to bad women. I'm afraid he won't be able to go up to heaven."

"Oh, no. Don't worry. I don't know what he did when he was young, but I know how he suffered in his last years. That suffering offsets everything. He surely will go to heaven. You don't need to worry about that. But if you are still worried, I will chant a sutra for heaven. Listen."

> Gero, gero, gero, gero, Nanmaidah.
> Gero, gero, gero, gero,
> Gokku-RAKku, gokku-RAKku
> Chiiin!!

"Well, your husband did many wrongs in his life. Just to make sure, I will chant again."

> Gero, gero, gero, gero, Nanmaidah.
> Gero, gero, gero, gero,
> Gokku-RAKku, gokku-RAKku
> Chiiin!!

Old Mrs. Gecko was relieved and went back home.

昔

The Frog Priest counted. "Three more. Who will come next?"

He waited. But nobody came. The afternoon passed. Soon the sun was going down. But still nobody came. "It's strange. There should be three more."

There came a young cicada. "Frog Priest, Frog Priest, I was singing with my buddy. Suddenly he stopped, fell down from the tree, and passed away. I was always with him. We came out of the ground together, molted together, got married together, looked for food together. We thought we would die together too, but he just went alone. I hope he will go to heaven. Please chant a sutra for heaven for him."

The Frog Priest chanted,

> Gero, gero, gero, gero, Nanmaidah.
> Gero, gero, gero, gero,

Gokku-RAKku, gokku-RAKku
Chiiin!!

The young cicada said, "Thank you very much." He started to fly off.

"Wait a minute!" said the Frog Priest. "You said that you and your friend came out of the ground together, molted together, and got married together. If you were born at the same time, you don't need to worry. You will go up to heaven with him by tonight. Yes, you will. I will chant a sutra for heaven for you, too."

Gero, gero, gero, gero, Nanmaidah.
Gero, gero, gero, gero,
Gokku-RAKku, gokku-RAKku
Chiiin!!

"I chanted it for you. You will surely go up to heaven soon."

The young cicada flew off.

昔

After that, nobody came. The sun was almost set. Soon the day would be over. The Frog Priest sat on a leaf and waited, looking this way and that way.

"Will somebody come from this way, or that way?"

While he was waiting, rowdy boys were playing around the pond. They threw stones into the pond. One of them hit the frog's head.

He said, "*Kyu!*" and fell into the pond, and never came up.

Nobody chanted a sutra for the frog.

So I don't know whether he went up to heaven or down to hell.

There was no one to chant a sutra for the frog. Will he go up to heaven or down to hell?

Will you help me chant for him?

> Gero, gero, gero, gero, Nanmaidah.
> Gero, gero, gero, gero,
> Gokku-RAKku, gokku-RAKku
> Chiiin!!

Oshimai

昔

COMMENT FROM MRS. FUJITA: Once when I finished telling this story, saying that I didn't know whether he went up to heaven or down to hell, a child chanted the sutra for the frog. He said he felt pity if the frog couldn't rise to heaven after all the chanting he did for other animals. Another child told me that even if I didn't know, God keeps an eye on everything, and the frog would surely be sent to heaven by God.

Behind the house where I grew up there was a pond, and there were many red frogs in the pond. We caught them, skinned them, gutted them, grilled them, and ate them. It was a time of food shortage, and we lived at the price of the frog's lives. At that time, I could do that. But in science class in high school, I could not do the frog dissection at all. When students threw away those dissected bodies in trash cans, I felt very sorry for the frogs.

My Uncle in the Farm taught me, "The only time you can kill living things is if you connect them into your life."

昔

The place where good people go, after their death, is called differently depending on religions. In Japanese Christianity, it is called *Tengoku* (Heaven).

In Buddhism, it is called *Gokuraku*. In Shinto religion, I think it is called *Josei*.

I had a friend who was devoted to Christianity. Her husband, like an average Japanese, didn't think very much of religion, but I assume he believed he would go to Gokuraku. But when he died, my friend decided to hold his funeral with her priest reading the Bible for him. So he went to Tengoku. When my friend died, her son was still young. He asked his relatives for help and they held her funeral at the Buddhist temple. So she, a devoted Christian, went to Gokuraku.

They were a loving couple. Whenever I tell this story, I remember them.

TIP FROM FRAN: When you tell this story, it's fun to distinguish each animal character by different postures and voices. For instance, for the Frog Priest, stick your elbows out and place your hands palm-down in front of your waist, imitating a frog's bandy legs.

American audiences of all ages enjoy chanting the frog sutra with the story. But when I think they will do better with a simpler version, we just chant "Gero, gero, Gokku-RAKku" three times. Chiin!

GLOSSARY & PRONUNCIATION GUIDE

Japanese pronunciation is very clear, and no sounds are skipped over. Every syllable (consonant+vowel) gets its own equal beat. Each doubled consonant or extra vowel gets an additional beat. Even "n", the only single consonant, gets a beat in songs and poetry.

The vowel sounds are similar to Italian or Spanish:

a as in "father"

e as in "pet"

i as in "ski"

o as in "so"

u as in "rude"

Japanese words are in italics followed by their pronunciation, showing stressed SYLlables in UPper CASE. If it's all lower case, please try to say the whole word flat. Literal translations follow pronunciation tips in brackets.

Amitabha a MI ta ba: The principal Buddha in the Pure Land sect, often called "The Buddha of Infinite Light."

Apprentice: A person receiving on-the-job training and lessons in exchange for his work.

Basama BA sa ma: an older woman; Grandmother.

Botamochi bo TA mo chi: A sweet snack: ball of half-pounded rice covered with azuki bean jam.

Buddha: The Enlightened One, founder of Buddhism.

Butterbur: plant with large rhubarb-like leaves *Petasites japonicus.*

Choja CHO ja: Rich man, self-made millionaire.

Daikon DA i ko n: A mild-flavored winter radish *Raphanus sativus* with a very long white root.

Edo E do: The former name of Tokyo, the seat of power for the Tokugawa shogunate that ruled Japan from 1603 to 1868.

Enma-sama E n ma-sa ma: Judge who decides whether souls go to heaven or hell.

Fukushima fu KU shi ma: Japanese Prefecture (state) in which Mrs. Fujita grew up.

Futon fu TO n: A Japanese bed; a mattress and thick quilts spread on the floor.

-*gami* ga mi: A suffix added to the name of a Shinto deity; *kami.*

Gokuraku go ku RA ku: Buddhist heaven; Paradise.

Gokkurakku gok ku RAK ku: The sound of a big frog croaking.

Jisama JI sa ma: An older man; Grandfather.

Jizo ji ZO: A Buddhist statue, made of stone.

Kami KA mi: One of the countless Shito deities; hair; paper.

Kannon-sama KA n no n-sa ma: The Goddess of Mercy, who was said to grant wishes. Also known as *Quan Yin.*

Kimono ki mo no [clothing]: A traditional long Japanese robe wrapped and tied with a sash.

Koban KO ba n: Large oval gold coin in Edo period feudal Japan, equal to about 1,000 yen.

Miso MI so: A savory thick paste made by fermenting soybeans with bran and salt, used as soup-base and seasoning for sauces and spreads, pickling vegetables or meats.

Mochi mo chi: Snacks made by pounding steamed short-grain gluti-nous rice into a smooth dough in a mortar. It is traditionally made in a ceremony called *mochitsuki*.

Mon MO n: A small coin in the old days, worth only a little.

Namu amida butsu NA mu A mi da BU tsu [Hail, Amida Buddha]: The most basic Buddhist sutra.

Nanmaida or **Nanmaidah** na n ma i da: The drone when people don't know their prayers or are mumbling.

Oban O ba n: An old time oval gold coin equal to about 10,000 yen.

Oni o NI: Ogres with sharp claws, wild hair, and two horns. Their skin may be red, blue, or other colors. When Japanese children play tag, the one who is "it" is called the Oni.

Oshimai! o shi MA i [It is closed]: Traditional story ending in Mrs. Fujita's Fukushima dialect.

Ryo ri yo: An old time oval gold coin equal to one koban, i.e. about 1,000 yen.

Sake sa ke: An alcoholic beverage distilled from fermented rice; rice wine.

-sama -sa ma: A very honorific suffix added to a name, comparable to "Sir or Ma'am."

Samurai sa mu RA i: The warrior class in old Japan.

-san -sa n: A polite suffix added to a name, comparable to "Mr., Mrs. or Ms."

Setsubun se tsu bu n: The day before the first day of spring, on the old lunar calendar.

Shoji SHO ji: A door, window or room divider consisting of translucent paper over a frame of wood which holds together a lattice of wood or bamboo.

Sumo su MO: Japanese wrestling.

Sutra: Buddhist scripture; prayer.

Tanuki TA nu ki: An Asian animal in the dog family *Nyctereutes procyonoides*, sometimes translated "raccoon dog" or—very misleadingly—"badger."

Tatami ta ta mi: Resilient floor mats, covered with woven straw.

Toshigami-sama to SHI GA mi sa ma [toshi year or age-gami god]: The Shinto god who delivers another year of life during New Year's Eve night.

Uwabami u wa ba mi: A monster snake

Zatobo-sama za TO bo sa ma: A blind priest; or a blind traveling entertainer, shaven-headed like a priest, who played shamisen, sang songs, and told stories.

BIBLIOGRAPHY

Endo, Toshiko. *Endo Toshiko no Katari* [The telling of Toshiko Endo].Transcribed and edited by Hiroko Fujita. Tokyo: Isseisha Publishing Company, 1995.
In this volume, Fujita preserved 200 folktales in colloquial Japanese from the repertory of a Fukushima elder. Unfortunately this rich resource is not available in English.

Fujita, Hiroko. *Katare Yamanba* [Speak! Mountain Woman] Volumes 1-7. Tokyo: Taihou-sha Publishing Company, 1996, 1997, 1998, 2000, 2003, 2004, 2006.

Ikeda, Hiroko. "A type and motif index of Japanese folk-literature." *Folklore Fellows Communications* No. 209 (FF), Helsinki: Suomalainen Tiedeakatemia, Academia Scientiarum Fennica, 1971.
Ikeda categorized and summarized, in English, the tales collected by Japanese folklorists, assigning tale-type numbers and Aarne-Thompson motif index numbers.

Mayer, Fanny Hagin, translator. *Ancient Tales in Modern Japan: An Anthology of Japanese Folk Tales*. Bloomington, IN: Indiana University Press, 1984.
In this book, Mayer provided full retellings of representative tales in English.

Mayer, Fanny Hagin, translator and editor. *The Yanagita Kunio Guide to the Japanese Folk Tale*. Bloomington, IN: Indiana

University Press, 1986.

Here, Mayer translated Yanagita Kunio's scholarly analysis *Nihon mukashibanashi meii* (1948), providing the tales in synopsis form with his detailed notes about local variants.

Stallings, Fran (editor), Harold Wright, & Miki Sakurai (Contributors). *Folktales from the Japanese Countryside: As Told by Hiroko Fujita*. Santa Barbara: Libraries Unlimited, 2007.

CITATIONS AND ADDITIONAL NOTES

These stories were translated and adapted from Mrs. Fujita's telling in Fukushima dialect, as transcribed by her followers "The Young Yamanbas" and published in *Katare Yamanba* (Speak! Mountain Woman) Volumes 1-7.

Each story title, in English, is followed by the Japanese title in italics. Then comes the volume and page reference: KY 7.082 means it starts on page 82 of *Katare Yamanba* Volume 7.

If a comparable tale was collected by Japanese folklorists, its index number in Ikeda (1971) or Mayer (1986) comes next. Note: these classification numbers follow a different system from Aarne-Thompson, nor do they match the numbers assigned by other Japanese folklorists.

Although Mayer lists the Prefectures in which tales were collected, she often doesn't mention Fukushima for a tale that Mrs. Fujita knows. It seems the folklorists didn't interview Mr. Takeda or Mrs. Endo. And quite a number of Mrs. Fujita's stories can't be found in the folklorists' indexes. They may be unique to Miharu village.

VILLAGERS

Contest of Silence *Damarikko Kurabe.* KY 7.082, Ikeda 1351A.

Note from Fran: Variants on motif J2511 "silence wager" appear worldwide. Get Up & Bar the Door!

Crane and Tortoise *Tsuru Kame.* KY 1.111.

A Couple Married on Koshin Day *Koshinsama no Hi ni Shugen o Ageta Hito Hanashi.* KY 6.071; Stith Thompson Motif J210.

Unhappy Daughter-in-Law *Yome no Kusatori.* KY 5.099.

Two in One Bite *Hitokuchi Futatsu.* KY 7.008a.

Sewing Lesson *Momohiki w Jozu ni Nuenai Hanashi.* KY 7.008b.

Eavesdropping Mother-in-Law *Yome no Furuino.* KY 7.010.

Poisoning Mother-in-Law *Shuutome no Dokusatsu.* KY 7.012, Ikeda 1448.

An Offering Withdrawn From Buddha *Hotoke no osagari.* KY 5.094.

Please *Onegai.* KY 6.168.

The Price of Three Stories *Hanashi Senryou.* KY 7.112, Ikeda 910B, Mayer 174.

TRICKSTERS

Fleas on a Skewer *Nomi no Kushizashi.* KY 4.027.

COMMENT FROM MRS. FUJITA: I learned this story from Toshiko Endo. In her telling, Basama was very greedy and funny. I try to tell it the same way.

The Bridge Officer *Hashi Yakunin.* KY 1.069.

Horse Dengaku *Uma no Dengaku.* KY 4.061.

COMMENT FROM MRS. FUJITA: I learned this story from Uncle Kuni in the field. Later, I heard it from Toshiko Endo, too. In Endo's version, the story continues a little more. The official says, "I'm not talking about horse Dengaku! I'm talking about *ni-tsuketa uma* (loaded horse)."

Then Jisama fools him again, saying, "Oh, not Dengaku. You are talking about *nitsu-keta uma* (cooked horse)." Jisama is a cut, or two cuts, above the official.

A Love Potion and a Pharmacist's Wife *Yakushyu ya no Okami-san.* KY 5.078.

A Greedy Pharmacist *Tsuki Soi Baa.* KY 5.080.

Offering Paid Back Double *Saisen Baigaeshi.* KY 7.049.

A Horse that Dropped Gold *Kogane o Hiru.* Uma KY 7.070, Ikeda 1539, Mayer 171.

Moratorium Order *Tokuseirei* KY 7.073.

FOXES

Tofu Seller and Fox *Tofuya to Kitsune.* KY 6.046.

Aramaki Salmon *Aramakijake.* KY 6.041.

Samurai and Jisama *Samurai to Jisama.* KY 6.040, Ikeda 145C.

A Fox Apprentice *Kitsune no Kozou-san.* KY 5.016.

Old Man and Grateful Fox *Jisama to Kitsune.* KY 6.056.

Homesick Bride and Helpful Fox *Yomesama to Kitsune.* KY 2.076.

ONI

In With Oni *Oni wa Uchi.* KY 2.028.

Setsubun. KY 1.058, Ikeda 2026.

Danjuro Enma. KY 6.197.

KAPPA

Kappa's Cream *Kappa no Kouyaku.* KY 3.081, Ikeda 47C part II.

Sumo Wrestling With Kappa *Kappa no Hanashi.* KY 5.032, Ikeda 47C.

MANY GODS

The God of Age *Toshigami-sama*. KY 1.035.

Apologizing Crow *Karasu no Wabinaki*. KY 6.009.

Eighteen Years to Live *Jyumyo Jyuhachi*. KY 6.193, Ikeda 930D elements, Mayer elements in 185 parts II & III.

No Gods Here *Kami ga Nai*. KY 2.091.

JIZO

Talking Jizo *Monoiu Jizo*. KY 6.191.

Red Face Jizo *Akatsura Jizo*. KY 6.188.

Monkeys' Jizo *Saru Jizo*. KY 6.089, Ikeda 179B, Mayer 139.

KANNON

A Dream Millionaire *Yume Choja*. KY 5.065.

Lizard and Scarab *Kanachoro to Kanabun*. KY 7.084.

TRAVELING PRIESTS

A Visitor on New Year's Eve *Otoshi no Kyaku*. KY 6.078, 6.075, Ikeda 750B-3, Mayer 75.

A Blind Visitor on New Year's Eve *Zatobo-sama*. KY 6.075 Ikeda 750B-1.

Daishi and Forked Daikons *Kaishikosama to Futamata Daikon*. KY 6.148.

Covering Snow *Atokakushi no Yuki*. KY 6.149.

Kobo Spring *Kobo Shimizu*. KY 6.153, Ikeda 751A-2.

Kobo and Stone Potato *Kobosama to Ishi-imo.* KY 6.158, Ikeda
751A-3

UNCANNY TALES

Gourd Pool *Hisagobuchi.* KY 7.061, Ikeda 480E, 681.

Extracting Grease *Aburatori.* KY 6.117, Ikeda 956A, Mayer 99, 223.

Yamanji and the actor Yamanji. KY 7.157.

Mr. Red Cat *Aka-Neko Don.* KY 3.036, Ikeda 215B, 216B. Mayer
112-113 (Cat mountain).

COMMENT FROM MRS. FUJITA: I used the expression *"Omatsu osohka"* (Attack Omatsu) or *"Oharu osohka"* (Attack Oharu) in this story, but I've heard many times the wording *"Omatsu yarohka, Oharu yarohka."* *Yaru* can mean either "to kill" or "to rape." They say all red striped cats are male. So I might say this story came from a tale warning young girls against young men from a nearby village, who tried to steal women. Well, this is another flight of my imagination.

Ghost with Dignity *Fuukaku no Aru Yuurei.* KY 3.050.

ANIMALS

Two Rival Snakes *Hebi no Kuiai.* KY 1.010.

Messenger & Serpent *Hiyaku to Uwabami.* KY 1.015.

The Frog Priest *Kaeru no Bousama.* KY 3.016.

CONTRIBUTORS

Hiroko Fujita is a traditional *ohanashi obaasan* (storytelling grandma). She spent her childhood in the rural mountain town of Miharu in Fukushima Prefecture, where she heard hundreds of ancient folktales from village elders. A graduate of Japan Women's University who was an early childhood education for five decades, she now travels Japan, teaching young mothers the old tales. The author of thirty-one books in Japanese, she lives in Kashiwa, Chiba Prefecture, Japan.

Fran Stallings, a professional storyteller based in Bartlesville, Oklahoma, interpreted for Mrs. Fujita's twelve storytelling tours of twenty-two American states, Japan and Singapore. Stallings edited and adapted English translations of Mrs. Fujita's storytelling handbook *Stories to Play With* (August House, 1999) and a collection of forty-seven tales known throughout Japan, *Folktales from the Japanese Countryside* (Libraries Unlimited, 2008). Stallings' other publications include articles, stories, songs, and four CDs. Her academic training in biology informs her environmental work as "EarthTeller."

In 2003, Fujita and Stallings received the National (U.S.) Storytelling Network's International StoryBridge ORACLE Award for their work on both sides of the Pacific. They hope that these books will make Mrs. Fujita's stories available to English-speaking story lovers everywhere.

Translator Makiko Ishibashi attended the University of Tokyo. She lived in St. Louis while her husband did postdoctoral work and their two sons attended American schools. Now their sons are grown, and she lives in Saitama, Japan, with her husband. Her current interest is in the *ukiyoe* (woodblock prints) of Hiroshige, and Edo (the old name for Tokyo). She blogs bilingually at "A Hundred Views Of Edo"

If you have enjoyed the telling of—and discussion of—
Japanese folktales by Fran Stallings, please take some
time to visit:

www.franstallings.com
www.parkhurstbrothers.com
www.storynet.org